T0194249

Through the Valley

ELLEN KORTHUIS

WESTBOW
PRESS®
A DIVISION OF THOMAS NELSON
& ZONDERVAN

WestBow Press books may be ordered through booksellers or by contacting:

WestBow Press
A Division of Thomas Nelson & Zondervan
1663 Liberty Drive
Bloomington, IN 47403
www.westbowpress.com
1 (866) 928-1240

Because of the dynamic nature of the Internet, any web addresses or
links contained in this book may have changed since publication and
may no longer be valid. The views expressed in this work are solely those
of the author and do not necessarily reflect the views of the publisher,
and the publisher hereby disclaims any responsibility for them.

Any people depicted in stock imagery provided by Getty Images are
models, and such images are being used for illustrative purposes only.
Certain stock imagery © Getty Images.

ISBN: 978-1-9736-3072-2 (sc)
ISBN: 978-1-9736-3071-5 (hc)
ISBN: 978-1-9736-3073-9 (e)

Library of Congress Control Number: 2018906881

Print information available on the last page.

WestBow Press rev. date: 7/9/2018

Contents

Chapter 1

KARL SNAPPED THE LOCK ON the briefcase and, with his hands still resting on the new leather, stared through the lettering of the *Timberline* sign on the window. He needed time to say his private goodbyes to the predictable mountain town and the people who had woven themselves into the fabric of his life.

He would miss the colorless "Mornin', Karl" from his cronies at the ten o'clock coffee break. The dullness of the greeting was not an insult but an affirmation of his acceptance into that inner circle of men who gathered at the counter in Gordon's Café for midmorning socializing. Early on Karl had guessed the reason for his welcome into the group: he was a newspaperman, a writer, and to these friends that position was as mysterious and awesome as a president's place. If the truth was told, this elite bunch of the town's gentry was honored to drink their morning coffee with him.

They weren't a bashful bunch. They were as generous with their criticism as they were with their approval. This congress of aging town fathers readily gave his pride an occasional smack by frankly commenting on or openly disagreeing with his column. With time, he gathered that there was no meanness in fault finding; they, in their senior wisdom and experience, were only trying to set this young feller straight.

On this, his last morning, he hadn't expected backslapping—it wasn't their way—but the solemn silence had surprised him. A grin touched his face as he recalled the scene.

He'd seen Gordon, the spokesman, leaning against the shelving behind the counter, his sweatered arms crossed over his chest. Short, frayed pieces of yarn hung from the elbow where he'd caught it on the screen door, and his glasses, speckled with dust and water spots, had not concealed alert, twinkling eyes that promised the inevitable wit. When he spoke, Karl knew his place with them, and his leaving had been extensively discussed. "Karl, someday I'm going to write a book about you and me and this whole pitiful town. Some of it will even be true!"

Chuckles loosened the vocal chords, and at once everyone had words of advice. They admitted they would miss him, and he knew he'd be a part of the everyday conversation as long as anyone would remember to ask, "Heard from Karl lately?"

He'd said his goodbyes and now, as his eyes focused on the bold, precise letters of the newspaper's name, he wondered for the first time if old Bigelow had painted them.

Looks like his style, Karl thought.

The conclusion was meant as a compliment to the editor/owner of the local weekly—the man whose philosophy of work was as square and clear as lettering. But he was a bully!

The old fox would like that tag, because he could come back with "You need bullying!" And Karl, looking back, would agree with him. When the *Timberline* hired him, he'd been as green and naïve as a beginning writer could be, but Mr. Bigelow had accepted him on the grounds of a few articles and the evidence of and intense desire to write. That passion had been fueled by the wonder of translating thought into words, but the editor had often harped about his choice of words. "Don't say 'bright light,'" he'd bark. "Say 'blinding glare.' And don't say 'large group.' Say 'crowded room'!"

The white-haired, growling bear had taught, through merciless nagging, the pleasure of mobilizing words, but the memory of the constant badgering was clear as the muscles across his shoulders began to tighten. Unconsciously Karl nodded his head. It had been under the repeated threats from the giant's sharp tongue he'd learned there was not room in *Timberline's* tidy column for carelessly gathered details or lazy grammar.

The giant—all five feet, six inches of him—was so big that when you walked through the front door you had to fight for a spot, because his presence filled the room.

The young writer's fingers traced the three gold letters near the handle of the briefcase: AIR. *These should be my initials*, he thought. *But true to form, Bigelow had chosen this conspicuous place to send along a reminder of what he expects of me!*

On every desk, over the layout table, the phone, and over everything were the words "Accuracy! Integrity! Reliability!"

"Put some fresh AIR into the newspaper business," commanded his staff.

As Karl lifted the case, the shadowed letters of *Timberline* slid off the leather to his desk and lay there. Reluctantly he looked down at them and whispered, "Thanks, Mr. Bigelow, sir. *Auf Wiedersehen.*"

Without looking back, he walked to the door and then out into the street.

The inside of the car was hot. From the driver's seat, he stretched his long frame across the seat to roll down the passenger window, and as it disappeared into the door, he wished he could fill the vehicle and take with him the voices and feelings of this place. Settling himself, he pulled the door shut with a bang. "Might as well punctuate the fact that I'm about to pull out. Everybody already knows, but now they can always remind each other what time I left!"

The lines around his eyes and mouth relaxed into a contented smile as he enjoyed the slow drive along the one block of Main Street. The Closed sign hung in the barbershop window, and in a few minutes, the owner of the only gas station would lock up and walk home for supper. Gordon had pulled the shade on the store's front door to signal he'd gone for the day.

And now, Karl thought, *I'm going home too, but for the last time, and to say goodbye.*

The cliché that a good thing isn't appreciated until it's gone crossed his mind, but he knew it wasn't right to apply that line to his leaving. He'd valued his home long before today, with a gratitude that came from knowing there was a comfortable, congenial place to go after work. He would truly miss it and his friends.

When Mr. Bigelow had hired him, word passed around town that his young assistant needed a place to live. When Kirstin had come into the office with an offer of a room and two meals a day—"A nice, big bedroom with a view, and breakfast and dinner with my husband, Jon, and me," she'd explained—the old man had encouraged Karl to move right in. After Kirstin left the office, Mr. Bigelow filled in the details with fact and editorializing. "Jon, Kirstin's husband, is the new doctor. Been here about four years. She's a flighty sort but not featherbrained. You'd call her enthusiastic or energetic or some peer kind of word. They live at the top of the hill."

When Jon and Kirstin had offered a bedroom and place at their table, the initial plan had been the provision of board and room. The change had come so quietly he couldn't pinpoint when he'd gone from friendly renter to welcomed companion. And yes, the more recent change had slipped up on him too.

A feeling of resentment welled up as he grudgingly acknowledged that the events of the past few months had changed this home from a haven to a needed refuge. And apart from all that had happened, he detested having been robbed of the comfort of that haven.

All that had happened!

An unwelcome anger smoldered as he rolled over in his mind how he'd been forced to relive a time of tragedy and terror, how he and Anna had to once more struggle to stay alive, how they had been unable to ask friends for help, and how during that time he'd found it impossible to even confide in anyone. All this upheaval because of one man—this one who was owned by evil and driven by a passion to destroy him and Anna. Karl could feel the fear and tension gripping his mind and body.

Slow down. Back off.

Resisting the growing panic, he silently prayed, *Father, forgive me for allowing these feelings to blot out what you've done for us. Thank you for doing for us what we could not do for ourselves.*

"It's over," Karl said aloud.

Tonight, at home and before the farewells, he would at last be able to tell the story that he had needed to keep secret. For Jon and Kirstin, he'd start at the beginning, and then truly—surely—that part of his life would be finished.

He and Anna, suffering the ravages of postwar Germany, had survived, and that was all that mattered. But survival again had become their priority, their everyday way of life or death.

As he completed the turn that started the climb to the top of the long hill, his eye caught the silver sticker on the dash. "He is able."

From the day he'd first bowed his heart and knees to God, he'd been learning the vast scope of the Almighty's ability. Even now, as his thoughts bounced between past and present, his conviction was firm that this eternal Ruler was also his compassionate heavenly Father, and no matter what the past had been or what the years ahead might bring, the most coveted goal was to deepen and enjoy this relationship with a gracious God.

These thoughts prompted the question "Isn't this relationship exactly what life is all about?" His whole being responded with an affirmative, but then, as if turning from a glimpse of heaven to a view of the world, he thought, *Regretfully, the presence of our living God does not bar the existence of wickedness.* But now danger from this evil was over, and Karl vowed the memory would fade.

The drive from town to the turnoff took three minutes: one to the top of the long hill and two to where he'd leave the pavement. There were always sixty seconds of anticipating the waiting panorama and knowing that, whatever the season, the view would be spectacular. It seemed incredible that one person could see so much all at once. The winding valley—more like a canyon dotted with homes and stores—lay below, and rising behind and beyond was range upon range of mountains. The near ridges, green and tree covered, melted into the blues and purples of faraway peaks. Sunlight highlighted cliffs and granite faces, and this afternoon the distant valleys lay mysterious in the encroaching shadows.

The massive bulk of the heights and depths stirred in Karl the familiar feelings of finiteness and, at the same time, well-being. The sight reenforced his sense of kinship with the Creator.

The view passed out of sight, but the pleasure of it stayed with him until he turned into his lane.

Then—the sound of gunfire! He ground the brake pedal to the floor and pressed his body against the steering wheel. The choking grip turned his knuckles white, and the relaxed lines of his face sunk to deep grooves and bulges over tightly closed eyes. In that instant, grotesque and ugly faces, shots, screams, and falling figures flashed—pulsed—across the screen in his mind. But then, like an intrusion into this whirlpool of panic, the cause of the gunshot sounds registered.

Gravel! It was the new rocks spread over the driveway that were flying up and peppering the underside of the car. Stones hitting the car! Even with the relief of realization, Karl sat still for a long minute, unable to exhale. A scowl squeezed his face, and his hands lay limp against the wheel. His breath came out in a shudder and with it the words "Can't he stay dead?"

Chapter

2

SUNSET COMES EARLY IN THE mountains, and Kirstin already had the kitchen light on. As Karl walked slowly from his car, he could see her moving about. He knew before he opened the door the radio would be playing.

"Sometimes this part of the day gets too quiet, so I need a little noise," she had explained.

Karl knew too that Jon wouldn't be home yet, because he stayed in the office until six, and if he left on time, there was the fifteen-minute commute.

The *if* part was the cause of irregular dinner hours, but unless there was an emergency, the doctor would be on time—especially this night. That these best friends had been protected from any involvement in the experiences seemed a miracle, Karl knew that. Although Kirstin had come to some conclusions, even *she* had much to learn about the whole story.

"Hullo," Karl called.

"Hello yourself," she said with a smile.

She moved from the stove to pour him a cup of coffee. Setting the mug before him, she explained, "Jon will be a little late." Then, carefully, she asked, "Do you like the mugs?"

Karl looked down at the table and then over to the cup rack and nodded his head. She knew the nod didn't mean *I like the mugs* but *You did the right thing.* The others, the ones that had hung there a few days ago, had been a gift from the German salesman. A mocking gift. Karl remembered the first time he'd seen them lying in the box in the red tissue paper. Strange how he could recall every detail of those scenes. He hoped she had destroyed them. He would have enjoyed smashing each one himself.

"Yes, you were right to remove those reminders." Karl, and now Kirsten, wanted only to forget.

Except for the music, the kitchen—with its bright cupboards and shiny floor—was quiet. Both people had dropped into a private circle of thought that left the kitchen and companion unnoticed.

The hum of the opening garage door was the signal to look, first at each other and then at the kitchen door. Kirstin and Karl had shared a moment of differing feelings, but added to Karl's emotions was a sudden tense reluctance to relive, even in words, his past. In just a few minutes he would resolve the mystery surrounding the present by revealing the terror of the past.

After a hurried greeting, Kirstin handed Jon a mug of coffee, and they sat down. She was fidgety with anticipation, but Jon—his eyes looking first at Kirstin and then at Karl—said, *"Well?"*

Karl began.

Chapter

3

THE LOW, ALMOST FLAT LAND of the North German Plain is laced with waterways draining into the northern seas. Great fertile strips of farmland are separated by the rocky heath lands, and in these wedges of sand and gravel, trees grow. The green of wheat and oats, the pastures and fields for the dairy and hog farms, and the borders of trees give expression of quiet, pastoral life. Even the weather works to make the land pleasant, with the west winds off the North and Baltic Seas warming the land in winter and cooling the area in summer.

Topographical maps show the upper third of Germany as the Northern German Plain, but there is another division not drawn on that kind of map. At first it was an invisible line, drawn from north to south, that fractured this pleasant plain into two lands: East and West Germany. Later it became a visible barrier.

At the end of World War II, Great Britain, the United States, France, and the Soviet Union took authority in Germany, and at that time the country was divided into four areas of military occupation. The USSR soon began organizing a communist government and economic system in its zone, and when the Allied countries proposed a united Germany, the Soviet Union blocked their plans. The result of this dispute split the country into two sections: the free Federal Republic of Germany and the communist German Democratic Republic—or West and East Germany.

The War left ruin in every part of the land. Cities, farms, and industry had been destroyed, and not only had the army suffered devastating casualties but civilians died by the thousands.

One of the strange and pathetic consequences of that warfare was the surviving masses of desolate children. Some were temporarily separated from parents, but more often they were orphaned. To these waifs the term *postwar* meant little. For although the fighting was officially over, the suffering didn't stop. There were no safe homes, no loving families, and—too often—not enough food. These were dark years in German history for children and adults.

Across the sea and to the north of this distressed land lay another country which bore the scars of war. The unrelenting arm of Hitler's wartime Germany had reached up and wounded the country of Denmark.

In April of 1940 German forces invaded, and after only a few hours of fighting, the Danes surrendered, but theirs was not a whipped-dog submission. Behind that uneasy capitulation there sprouted and grew a heroic defiance. In 1943, the Danish Freedom Council was organized to lead the resistance movement. Indeed, those secret fighters blew up their own factories and transportation facilities, but for many of the warriors the most urgent responsibility was not to destroy ... but to save.

In defiance of the occupier's edict, nearly 7000 Jews were hidden and then—like some costly contraband—smuggled out of Denmark and across the sea to Sweden. But the resistance was costly. Thousands of policemen and resistance fighters, along with Danish Jews, were arrested, imprisoned, tortured, and executed.

One of the Freedom Council members who'd survived the war was a now graying widow, Elsie Jansen. Her husband, Frederick, had lived through the fighting only to succumb to disease months after the end of the conflict.

"How we fought side by side," she would recall with pride, and then remember what Frederick had reminded her: "'We do not fight with guns, you and I; we fight with ideas and plans and our schemes.'" And so it was that they had fought and won. At least they had succeeded often enough to encourage Elsie to reminisce about their use of wit against weapons. She was thankful the bloody war was over, but in the months that followed, she'd become aware of a grave danger that still existed to the south.

Word had come from across the North Sea of pockets of resisters and Jews caught inside the newly organized East Germany. It was these people—once hated and hunted by Nazis who were now targets of communism.

Sitting over a late evening supper of thinly sliced bread and fish, Widow Jansen visited with her friends and allies, James and Caroline Christiansen. It wasn't the first time they'd discussed the plight in East Germany, but tonight there was new information. Whispers passing from an informant gave sketchy details of an escape route being arranged. This time the destination was not Sweden but Denmark, and the landing was the tiny area of Falster.

Barely 30 miles separated a point on the coast of East Germany and this dot of free land. Yes, the three agreed, even if the waters of Mecklenburg Bay were patrolled by the Red Navy, these sailors were not God. They could not be everywhere at once. Surely it would be possible for those involved to carry their precious cargo to safety. A little boat with a small motor and two or three people would not attract attention.

Memories of their former exploits were vivid, and the past members of the Freedom Council talked about this present crisis as if they were part of it. Something of the old excitement made their voices crackle with enthusiasm as all three began to visualize how this intrigue was possible. As they parted, they agreed to discreetly inquire more about it.

Two weeks later, when the three met to share their collection of information, the Christiansens told Mrs. Jansen that the escape route's checkpoints were orphanages.

"Orphanages!" barked the lady. "How could they use such vulnerable places? That would involve children—innocent, guileless children, who could be hurt or who could unintentionally ruin the plan. There *must be* a better way!"

There were no living children from her marriage, but because of the cruelty of war, her heart had a deep tenderness for the young victims of adult conflict.

Elsie didn't know why she felt sad. It was the sort of weighty feeling that invaded with expecting the undesirable inevitable. She'd had the same sense when the doctor told them Frederick had only months to live. Even now she could hear her Fritz chide, "You can't always walk with the wind to your back."

She sat in the glow of the lamp and thought she felt an icy blast hit her face and her heart. It brought an involuntary shiver.

James broke into her thoughts "There is more to tell."

Elsie raised her head and looked at the speaker. His features were vague in the dimness, and she wiped at the tears in her eyes, hoping to sharpen the image. At that moment, she felt old—and alone—and did not want to think of anyone else's problems. She plucked at a thread on the worn tablecloth, picking and poking as if persistent determination would remove it. The weight of dread fell around her like a cape.

He continued, "Those who are doing this work need help. They have outlined for me how we three could fit into their plan. To tell the truth, we would not only fit in … we would be the final link. *Ja*, we would be stationed at the last stop in East Germany before the refugees take the boat across the Kadet Channel. I said to them, 'How could we enter the country undetected? What would we do?' They told me they have a farmhouse and a few buildings close to the coast. It's so close they feel that they can get us in safely.

"We would not travel overland any distance. There would be someone to bring pigs, cows, and chickens, to make the place look like a real farm. The house would be furnished for an orphanage, and of course," he raised his bushy eyebrows, "we would be supplied with orphans. After all, if we are to be orphanage keepers, we must have children, *ja*? My German is good, and if you and Caroline would act like two shy *fraus*, I could do whatever talking we need."

Elsie raised her hand, protesting his long speech.

"Stop! You talk like we are already going. How do you know we can do this? And you, Caroline, what do you think of all of this?" She waved her hand as if pushing away invisible objects. "Don't you think we are getting too old for this ..." She stopped, searching for the right word, and ended with "commitment?"

Caroline looked straight into Elsie's eyes and said, "We have arranged for a boat to get us across the bay. All you need to take are clothes. No, Elsie, we are not too old. You will find we are *just right*. You, James, and I are experienced in outwitting the enemy."

Frowning, Elsie murmured, "You have James. I have no one." She toyed with a small, metal-hinged box, opening and closing the lid. The figures on the embossed cover were richly clothed in heavy robes and hats. Silently she stared at them. The design depicted some sort of a festival, with a large, robed man giving a speech to the observers. She seemed to be engrossed studying the scene, but without raising her eyes, she spoke: "A matter of hours to get my clothes ready."

It was a statement, not a question. The husband and wife watched, and by her slow, purposeful movements, they knew what decision she'd made. She leaned back in her straight wooden chair and with measured, deliberate action, folded little pleats in the loose fabric of her apron and with the same definite gesture smoothed them away.

Grumbling to herself, she said aloud, "*Ja*, we are just right."

How, she thought, *had she made such a decision in moments, when she should have mulled it over for days?*

The words were heavy with resignation, but each of the three Danes knew following along behind these first feelings of fear and apprehension would be anticipation.

They had never needed to embellish the tales of their wartime exploits, for the memory of daring meetings, secret routes, and accomplished missions were sharply etched in their minds and borne out by scars from bullet wounds and broken and mended bones. But they had lived through it all, and this night those memories provided the courage to once more be "committed."

To the Christiansens, Elsie said, "I am no longer a fearless woman; I am like a fearful grandmother." She paused and sat quietly, struck by an inspiration. "We'll call that orphanage *Bestamar*. No, we won't paint a sign and hang it on the gate. No, no Danish signs, but in our hearts the orphanage farm will have that lovely, comfortable name: Grandmother."

The last vestiges of misgivings and dread had disappeared; the Freedom Council members had committed themselves to the adventure.

Without incident, they made a crossing from Falster Island across the Kadet Channel of Mecklenburg Bay and to the point of land in East Germany. Following directions, the three easily found the place; it was just as the information had promised. The farmhouse was furnished with a large wooden table, several chairs, simple cots ... and children. A cow, pigs, and chickens shared an area behind what was left of a barn. A waiting farm hand greeted them and briefly outlined their work. While they settled their belongings in the house, the man disappeared. They were on their own with nine children and a hopeful plan.

The opinion of the Danes was that the operation would be temporary, for they were sure those who wanted—or were able—to leave East Germany would speedily find their way through the underground and out to freedom.

Chapter

4

As DAYS SPREAD INTO WEEKS, a measure of confidence and peace came to the little farm. The escape route was working effectively. Their part of the intrigue was simple. A brief message delivered by a passing farmer would alert them that a stranger was on the way. Whatever preparations were needed were woven into the usual farm chores, but even then, the arrival of a new person puzzled the children. Christiansen explained he'd hired a new man, or if the person was a woman she was "someone to help in the kitchen."

After the first few "workers" had come and gone, the children did not question the procedure. It was just another temporary arrangement in their unsettled lives. These people would stay a day or a week and then leave as they had come, without greeting and without farewell. To the adult occupants of the farm it seemed the clandestine arranging of peoples' lives barely touched the outward appearance and workings of the orphanage.

Perhaps because the terrible wartime was over and the present escape plan was working successfully, no one suspected how swiftly it was going to end. If there had been screaming sirens or marching feet, someone would have felt the impending danger and made preparations, but the only clue to anything out of the ordinary was the black car that growled up to the gate. No one, even with this unusual appearance, could have guessed the outcome.

That day there was only one Jewish refugee, and he was disguised as a plain farm worker. Even if he'd looked out of place on the farm, there would have been no inquiries from the occupants of the black car.

It was wash day, and one of the two children assigned to the task was Karl Mann. Helping with the chores gave him a measure of security. Two brothers had died as soldiers and, as the other children, he awoke each morning hoping this would be the day his parents would find him. He was tall for his 12 years, and because of his sturdy build he was often called to work the extra hours or bear added responsibility. But he didn't complain, because despite the harsh lessons of war, Karl was learning to protect his character from the single motivation of personal survival.

James had seen him at mealtime hide away a crust of bread to be shared later with the half-starved cur that cowered in the trees behind the barn. Sometimes during evening prayers, if a small child whimpered from loneliness or fatigue, it would be Karl who cradled him into contentment. At times the orphan's caretakers worried that the boy's tender heart would not be bold enough to withstand what a postwar world might thrust at him. If James could have known the adult Karl, he'd have been more then reassured that the gentleness grew out of an inner strength.

Almost from the first day at the orphanage, Karl's special friend became Anna Klein. Perhaps it was because she was nearest his age their friendship developed, but whatever it was that drew them together, the outcome was a mutual admiration. He found it easy to be kind to the dark-haired, brown-eyed girl, and Anna loved him for his concern.

At times she would shout, "Let me do it myself!" when he'd elbow her out of the way in an attempt to "help" her, or her eyes would flash, warning him not to give advice.

"Okay! Okay!" He'd back off and watch, sometimes wincing as she worked to prove her independence.

She knew she could hammer, hoe, or carry almost as much wood as he, and Karl admired her for it. But when the sun set and the shadows began to deepen, it was his stronger arm that rested reassuringly across her slender shoulders, and she gratefully accepted his nearness.

There were other children on the farm: a girl who thought she was eight years old and six younger boys and girls. Because none of them could remember celebrating a birthday or recall a birth date, each was given a new day, month, and year that seemed to fit his or her size.

"You may choose the day and the month, and we will decide the year," Elsie had told them. She smiled when each chose the current month. "Sly little chickadees! You can't all have birthdays this month. We must spread out the celebrations." And so the six were assigned other months. Karl, Anna, and the eight-year-old were then able to set their dates, because they knew either the exact numbers or remembered the right season of the year. Life was beginning to settle into some orderliness.

Chapter

5

THE DAY THE CAR CAME, Karl and Anna were filling and emptying washtubs. Laundry was done in the backyard when the weather was warm, and this was a pleasant day. As an adult, Karl would try to recall if it had been morning or afternoon, but the occasion had been indelibly recorded in his child's mind simply as "the day."

He remembered that Mrs. Jansen had stopped the washing machine to watch three men come through the gate. So many times had he heard the story of invisible "grandmother" sign that he half expected to see the men duck when they passed under its phantom height. As the men approached the work area, Karl set his bucket next to the washtubs and straightened. Only then was he aware that two of the three carried guns. These two wore neat trousers and jackets, but the one whose hands were empty wore a fine suit and a splendid hat. They could have been visiting dignitaries. Anna stopped what she was doing and moved closer to Karl, watching the small parade.

They were unaware how Elsie stood rigidly alert, instinctively preparing for the worst. With struggling control, she stretched her lips into a smile.

The man with the hat said, "Gather the children."

Elsie's face revealed her surprise. The words should have been in German, but the man spoke in English. She barely understood his request. In a whisper of faulty German, she said in Anna's ear, "Anna, get the children."

Anna heard Mrs. Jansen's voice, but it took the push of Elsie's hand to give her power to move. She backed a few steps, turned, and flew across the dirt yard.

The man looked at Karl and said, "How many adults live here?"

The tone of his voice did not alarm Karl, and innocently he answered, "Today, four."

"Get them."

The words were a command, but were not harsh. He would have used the same tone if he'd asked for a glass of water. Karl's eyes did not leave the man's face; instead he studied it as if searching for some reason for the group's presence. The man was not intimidated by the boy's stare, but when Karl moved his eyes from the man's face to Mrs. Jansen's, he saw the open grief and horror in the woman's eyes. Later he would realize how clever the man had been to ask a child for the number of adults, for knowing no reason to lie, the boy would tell the truth—"Today, four." The boy was confused. The smile on the carefully groomed man's face revealed nothing, and when he looked to Mrs. Jansen for confirmation of the command, he got only a stare from eyes that even a boy of twelve could tell were filled with fear.

"Go!" The command was repeated, and this time Karl went.

The children were coming from the house or barn, and with a word to one or two, Karl found out where the other adults were. No one hurried. He watched the retreating backs of his friends as they walked to where Mrs. Jansen stood and wondered if he should disobey the command and stay with her. She hadn't moved, not even to meet the children, nor had the unarmed man moved. He stood watching Karl.

The pressure from that steady look turned Karl toward the barn, and in minutes he returned with James, Caroline, and the temporary farmhand to join Elsie and the circle of children.

The three men stood waiting for the hesitant group to form. The smile faded from the speaker's face. But in the same even voice, he began to speak. The boy thought the man sounded like a king, or an emperor, addressing his subjects. He told the children to form a line facing him, and obediently they moved. Karl slid next to Anna, so his arm touched hers.

Mr. Christiansen's voice broke into the pantomime. "What are you doing? These are orphan children. What are you doing?" he repeated.

With each word it was as if he comprehended more of the situation and as he took a step forward the man's two companions raised the guns. James stopped. For a tense moment the only noises were the sniffles and whispers from the children. Karl and Anna watched with unblinking eyes.

The voice said, "You"—he looked at Mr. Christiansen—"and you, *Fraus.*" He stopped and, inclining his head toward the refugee, said, "And especially you, are a threat to this new country. You jeopardize the unity of the system, for you have no reason to hide and sneak out of the country. We will not tolerate those who will not cooperate with the progress. You must learn this lesson, as those who conspire with you will learn."

With a nod the two with guns fired seven shots. There were no sounds from the children—there had been no time. Too late the adults screamed and moved forward, but immediately the guns were pointed at them, and a cruel stillness pressed down over the grizzly mound of children spread over the ground

"Now," the man said, "you see what happens to innocent victims of conspirators. But," he explained in his too-smooth voice, "even though you have learned your lesson, there are those who plot with you who need to learn too. Just to relieve your minds, I will tell you the two older children will not die. They are our witnesses to your friends."

He stopped talking and took one step back. The guns cracked again, and eleven people lay dead. The whole world was silent. There were no voices, no sounds from the washing machine, no rustles from the leaves overhead; they hung limp as if ashamed.

Without a word to Anna and Karl, the three turned their backs and with long, sure strides reached the car and drove away.

Chapter

6

THE ONLY SOUND IN THE kitchen was the ticking of a clock. Jon and Kirstin sat unmoving, staring at their friend. How many times had they seen war movies with scenes similar to those Karl described? But watching them on plastic film had evoked a plastic response. At the time they'd had a sympathetic response, but soon they had forgotten the story. But now, to know someone who had suffered through the horrors of such brutality, to hear a minute-by-minute account, opened their eyes and touched their hearts. Because hurting and death were not strangers to Jon, he had vividly pictured the scene. His sympathy with the agony of the experience was real. Kirstin's cheeks were wet with tears.

"Karl, I'm so sorry," she whispered.

A full minute of silence passed. Kirstin couldn't trust her voice, and Jon was lost in thought. Karl sat motionless, watching the cold coffee in his cup. For months after the orphanage he and Anna had lived and slept with the scene always before them. In the daylight a black car or the resonance of a controlled masculine voice made them hold their breaths in fear.

In the night, bad dreams were made of handsome, well-dressed men and the trigger-fast flash of a gun. But mostly it was the voice. In the years that followed, a certain hum of car engine or a particular pitch on an organ would bring back the tone of the man's softly spoken words, and once again the sound of shots would ring in their ears. The remembrance of that voice remained, but finally the man's image blurred and faded. Time healed the pain of the memory, and Karl realized with a start that this was the first time he'd told a living soul the entire sequence of events. He hadn't realized the telling would call back an almost overpowering sensation of alarm.

Jon's touch made him jump. His head jerked up, and though his mind knew he would see his friend, his eyes first registered fear and then relief. Jon's hand rested on Karl's arm.

"Karl, did you ever feel toward those three men—the one in particular—as King David felt about his enemies? You know, David once asked God to knock out his enemy's teeth. He wanted revenge." Jon's thoughts had turned to a Psalm he'd read that morning; in it was the plea from Israel's great king asking God to shatter the gnashing teeth of those who wanted his destruction.

Jon's motive for the question was entirely serious, but the picture it conjured up in the minds of the listeners broke away the gloom that had filled the cozy kitchen.

Karl's eyes rested on his friend. "I honestly don't think I ever thought of revenge. If the circumstances had been different, I probably would have, but Anna and I spent the next few years, day and night, concentrating on survival."

Karl bowed his head and continued.

Chapter

7

IN THE YEARS THAT FOLLOWED the events at the farm, Karl and Anna became faithful friends. They accepted the loss of siblings and parents and in their place had adopted each other as family. There had been no one to sympathize with their loneliness or ease their difficulties, so armed only with the resilience of youth, they'd pushed ahead. Even if there had been family or friends, there would not have been the luxury of pampering, for the post-world war time was of rebuilding for the world and its people. Every nation was licking its wounds waiting for the destruction and grief to become fading scars.

Even a 12-year-old boy, recalling the black grief of the orphanage, concluded that if there was to be any escape from the communist state, it would be devised and carried out without help. And so Karl, with the cunning of a man-child, had found a way. The simplicity of the plan, and the unabashed confidence that it was possible, carried the two children from a desolate prison state, across a line, to a desolate free state.

It had taken many months to cover what would have been a 600-kilometer journey by road. Karl's plan had called for the obvious—they were to move slowly along as inconspicuous children. To hike purposefully along a road might have called attention to themselves, so by day the two wandered through the fields of the low, almost flat, North German Plain, but by night they returned to furtive refugees.

Caution prevented them from asking for food. Instead a farmer would discover a place where a few carrots had been dug from his garden, or later in the season, he would be missing potatoes. The two occasionally ate raw eggs.

There was always a bombed-out building, but unless the warning bark of a dog frightened them, they would make their way to a barn for shelter. A ruined structure would provide four walls, a floor, and parts of a roof, but on the cold nights the security of a warm hayloft helped make the daylight trek bearable.

Even those perilous days held a sprinkling of good memories. Cool brooks and meadow flowers brightened their way. Heading always west, they had covered many kilometers of the grasslands and river crossings on their meandering route when Karl began to find what he knew he had to watch for—indications that the border was near.

By now he had learned it was wiser to share with Anna some of their dangers and then listen to her suggestions or quiet her fears. At times they had made abrupt changes to their route because of obvious danger or an intuitive signal. Then, with a challenge or clever word, he had spared Anna from alarm. Most of the time he'd gotten away with his little deceptions, but as they'd neared the border he had known she must be aware of every plan and move. There must be no mistakes.

The night before they had covered the last kilometer, they'd found a small farm and a weary-looking old hay shed. The place seemed deserted; even what was growing in the garden appeared to be volunteers from a previous crop. Under cover of twilight, they'd used sticks to pry out some of the ragtag stand of vegetables: three carrots and a misshapen onion. The dirt was thick under their fingernails and stuck in small blobs to their hands and food, but even though there was a nearby well, they had not taken a chance on a squeaking or clanging pulley.

Karl matched Anna's slow step as they made their way to the shed. He carried the makings for their meager supper as she scraped

Through the Valley

at the mud under her nails. As best they could, they'd cleaned the vegetables by rubbing them with hay. Ever since he'd explained their position and what the next day might bring, she had not spoken a word, and Karl was worried. She'd been brave and strong, even when tired and hungry, and this solemn withdrawal added a new fear to his heart.

The three pieces of food lay on his open hand. Anna sat hunched, with her elbows resting on her bare knees. With the toe of her scuffed brown shoe made a pile of hay, and then with one quick twist of her ankle sent the small stack flying. She straightened, and Karl used the moment as his opportunity to offer her the biggest of the two carrots. She took it. Neither child bothered to scrape the dirt out of the tiny furrows, and as they chewed, they were oblivious to the sound of the sand grinding between their teeth. Anna's jaw still moved, but Karl had watched her put the larger half of her carrot in her pocket.

She was afraid! Some innate sense told him that Anna's present sullen preoccupation was a defense against crying or even speaking of her fear. Now, as a preparation for the unknown future, she was hoarding away a piece of light-yellow, deformed carrot.

The maturing, manly part of him had provided a special strength and energy for the next few hours. He was invigorated by the probability of their escape into West Germany. It was not a problem to foresee the advantage of working for survival in a country where they would not be hindered by the fear of being captured. For Karl, crossing the border meant that the possibility of life would be greater than the possibility of death.

Anna hadn't thought of that; she had only the knowledge that they were leaving familiar territory, however dangerous, to go a long way to unfamiliar places. She was willing to go because Karl said so, but her little-girl's heart was frozen by fear. Hunger hadn't produced the desire to eat, and there was no courage left to loosen her tongue.

Karl laid his carrot and onion on his lap and reached for Anna's hand. As if it was the thing to do, he pushed the too-long, frayed sleeve up off her thin fist, and with his slender fingers began to gently flatten her palm against his. At first Anna resisted, but then Karl firmly held her wrist, and with his thumb began to rub the back of her hand. He could feel the muscles slowly relax, and into the hush he began to hum a childish lullaby.

From where he sat he could look up through a window and see the last fading colors of daylight. For all his strength, there was something in the twilight hour that stirred a longing. If only there was a friendly noise to interrupt this solitude, something like the bark of a good dog or a hen's contented clucking. The ache for the call from a mother's voice had dulled, but a clue that the desire still lay in his heart was a long, heavy sigh.

When he thought he could trust Anna not to pull away, he removed one hand and slipped his arm around her shoulders, drawing her to him. He was aware of the silent tears that dropped to his shirt, but without stopping he continued his wordless song. No other sound invaded the stillness.

The barn was dark when Karl realized Anna was asleep. He laid her down across the hay and straightened his tingling arm. Now he ate. He held the onion while taking a bite of carrot, but even as he chewed, the desire for sleep overcame hunger, and so, with care, he put his share of food in his pocket and lay down on the hay. A curved slice of moon cast a vague shadow over the pair and showed that the sleep of children, even eager or anxious ones, is deep and sweet.

Karl was awakened, not by the usual predawn cold but by the touch of a determined wet tongue on his cheek and nose. He pulled the furry body to him, and even in the dullness brought about by deep sleep, he began to rub the flabby ears and soft head of a pup. Slowly comprehension came, and he sat up in the dull dawn light and looked at what his hands held. For just a second, the animal was still the two brown eyes looked at Karl's face, and then the little body burst into convulsive, happy wiggles.

Like a duet, Karl's laugh and the dog's yips filled the musty barn, and Anna stirred. For a few delicious minutes, caution was forgotten while the two children rolled and tumbled in the hay with the wiry mongrel—but a noise like a door slamming ended the play.

Even the pup, sensing the change, sat quietly licking Karl's hand. Except for its squirming to settle himself against Anna's leg, there was no movement or noise. The day was beginning to brighten, and while the children waited for some shape to appear at the door, they began to notice the furnishings of the room. To the side of the stacked hay was a stall with a manger and what appeared to be a small room closed off by a half door. The minutes crept by while the three sat quietly.

Finally, when no one came, Karl stood and peeked out the square window. Everything seemed the same as it had been when they'd walked from the garden to the barn the evening before. The house, abandoned and neglected. Ragged curtains flapped and caught on the broken window panes, and pieces of the roof's covering lay strewn across the cluttered, overgrown yard.

Turning, he whispered to his small companion, "It must have been a broken door banging in the wind." With that conclusion, the two children began to explore the barn.

They'd only gone a few steps when Anna stopped and grabbed Karl's arm. "Look! What is it!" she exclaimed.

A board had been laid across the manger, and on it was a dish and a scrap of paper. The plate was cracked and scratched, but on it was a stack of thick sliced bread, and next to it was something else. There were two generous portions and a smaller crust, each spread with a white buttery grease.

Lard, Anna guessed.

Karl picked up the top slice and found it was soft and had the smell of fresh-baked bread.

Who? How? When?

As delighted as the two were with the food, they had the uneasy feeling that they had not been, and were not even now, alone.

"Hullo?" Karl called out.

The only response to his voice was the dog's happy yip. Karl laid the bread back on the plate and picked up the small package. The soft contents were wrapped in a tattered cloth and tied with a length of old shoelace. Carefully he untied the knot and pulled back the fabric. There lay an identical supply of food.

Anna retrieved the paper from where it had fallen to the floor, and Karl read, *"Golt halten Ju."*

Someone knew they were in the barn, had probably seen them dig the vegetables, and perhaps this minute watching them. Could that person be in the house or maybe in a nearby cellar? Maybe even in this building? Whoever it was surely meant no harm, or they would have attacked in the dark night. And most of all, they would not have written "God bless you" and left a supply of food behind.

"Do you think someone sees us?" Anna asked, her eyes wide and questioning.

"Yes, but who, and why don't they come out so we can see them?" Karl asked.

"Maybe they don't want us to see them, and maybe they just want to give us something to eat because they like children," Anna surmised.

Karl looked at the three chunks of dark bread. One for him, one for Anna, and one, that crust with a smear of the grease—it was for the dog! The bread was for three; both stacks were for three. Did the giver mean that they were to take the dog as well as the food?

The night before, Karl had used much of that needed emotional reserve to comfort Anna, and today he would face his greatest challenge. Never in all his boyhood days had he known such a desperate need for reassurance as he felt that moment, standing in the rickety barn. He had to think that somewhere there was someone who liked children enough to risk helping them. Surely this bread and the pup were the signs that somebody cared.

His eyes filled with tears. He couldn't know, but he would find that it was the last time he'd need the outlet of weeping for years to come. As the tears spilled from his eyes and ran down his cheeks, their departure made room for the courage he'd draw on for the days ahead, the courage brought about by the assurance that someone cared.

Anna's fingers brushed away his tears, and it was her small hands that retied the string on the package. She dropped the treasure into Karl's jacket pocket and passed the plate of bread to him. All this was done in silence, but when each had their share in hand, Karl bowed his head and prayed. It was the voice of a child who—with that unique wisdom granted to children—understood and appreciated this gift of food.

"*Golt, halten uns.*"

Anna echoed, "God, keep us."

The pup, who had dropped down on his haunches, began to whine.

"Oh, you," Anna crooned. "You are hungry too?"

Karl broke the crust into four pieces. "We'd better give him a little at a time, or he'll be finished before we start!" And so the three ate, savoring every crumb of the dark bread and happily content that the food for the next meal was safely tucked in Karl's pocket.

"He needs a name," Anna stated.

"I think I have a good one. How about *Dritte*?" Karl asked.

"Dritte?" She laughed. "Why do you want to call a dog *Third*?"

"Well," Karl said, holding up two fingers, "first there were two—you and me—and now there are three. He's the third!" and he held up three fingers.

"Won't you feel dumb when you call for *Third* to come to you?" Anna asked.

"No. He's our dog, and if we call him *Third* it's because it means he's special to us. It's like he's part of the family."

So it was settled. The puppy became Dritte.

Chapter

8

THE THREE NEVER KNEW WHEN exactly they crossed the invisible line that divided East and West Germany, but when they stopped for the night, they fell asleep confident they were on the other side. The day's journey had been simple. Always heading west, they'd walked, or sometimes romped, through fields and down paths, and not one person had questioned their intentions or destination. Two children and a dog were a pleasant sight to the occasional farmer. Even to the patrol who watched through binoculars they were a moment of entertainment.

Somewhere south lay Frankfort. There wasn't a reason for the goal except Karl often heard the city's name in adult conversations and had concluded it was situated somewhere near the Rhine River. For most of his lifetime Germany had been at war, and though he had suffered, his loyalty to the homeland was strong. Now, being near Frankfort and the Rhine seemed a patriotic gesture.

The three travelers crossed the flat plain, hiked over the slopes of the central highlands, and eventually came into the southern hills of Germany. Many times people offered food and lodging to the trio. Their journey ended just north and east of Frankfort, where Karl hired on as a potato digger.

The sight of the two children and a dog coming down the road stirred Mr. Oldenburg's curiosity. Stopping his work and leaning on his hoe, he thought, *Pitiful.* That was his first impression, but as they drew nearer, he said to himself, *More pitiful!*

When they were just a few steps away, he called out, "Kids, where are you going?" To him it seemed logical they were passing through, since he knew every family around, and this boy and girl did not belong to any of them. Karl looked at the man. They had been watching him too, as they neared his farm. They drew up, and holding Dritte close, Karl surprised Anna by speaking with a grownup confidence. "We are looking for work. We have come a long way."

The farmer and this small group of refugees studied each other as Dritte begged to be put down.

"Let him run," Mr. Oldenburg said. Tentatively, Anna set the dog on the ground and watched him scamper to the farmer. He bent over and, rubbing the jumping dog's ears, said to Karl, "What kind of work can you do?"

"I can do lots of things. I am strong, and Anna is strong too," Karl declared.

Mr. Oldenburg, looking at the two thin, wretched waifs and made a decision that would change his life for years to come. He said, "I do need help harvesting my potato crop. Do you think you can dig potatoes?"

"Yes, sir," Karl replied.

"It is hard work. No play, just work," Mr. Oldenburg said with a frown.

Anna took a step back, showing Karl she was fearful of this man and his offer. She didn't speak, but her reaction told Karl how she felt.

Karl said, "Can we try out to see if we can do the work?"

A figure that had come out of the house came across the field and approached the group. She stood listening and watching the children. Who were these two? Where had they come from? Where were their parents? She saw Anna's retreat and wondered at her withdrawal. She had seen many wartime children, but these two were most to be pitied. She laid a hand on her husband's arm and nodded her head, and he looked from the children to her and replied with his own nod.

"Yes, you can try out. Come." And the four stepped over the potato plants onto the road to the house.

Mrs. Oldenburg opened the door and motioned the children to enter. She would have had them enter the house, but the two stayed in the doorway and stared. Here was a real kitchen, with a real table and chairs. There was a window with a curtain, and a stove with pans of bubbling food on the burners. As Anna clasped Karl's arm, Mr. Oldenburg, with his hand on Karl's back, gave a little push. The two moved into the room. Mrs. Oldenburg said, "Come, sit down." They did as bidden, and for the first time in many months, Karl and Anna sat at a kitchen table. As if unable to speak, the two sat silent, exploring the room with their eyes.

Mrs. Oldenburg turned to the stove, pretending to put food in serving dishes, but held her apron to her face to mop the tears that slid down her wrinkled cheeks. The tears sprang from bitterness … and sympathy. Her heart, broken by battering from the war, had grown bitter. Too much had been taken from them. Loyalty to the Reich had encouraged them to proudly offer their only child, a son, to fight for the supremacy of Germany. They had been so sure they were in the right, but as the war progressed they'd begun to question the brutality of Hitler's conquests. When news of Eric's death came, their world turned dark. All the sacrifices seemed for nothing, and sadly, the only goal on their horizon was survival. Each morning was just a repetition of the day before.

Today, as she stood in her own house, by her own stove, she felt a cleansing surge of sympathy. Here were mere children also battered by the ravages of war. By their faces, their clothes, and their attitude, they also had the goal she knew so well—survival. She dipped the big cup in the pot and ladled steaming potato soup into bowls.

As Karl and Anna ate, Mr. Oldenburg spoke as a thought came to his mind. Yes, they would put the two upstairs to the attic room. Yes, oh yes, they could keep their pup. Karl would work with him in the fields with the crop, and Anna could help Mrs. Oldenburg with canning and cooking. Even as he laid out the plan, misgivings about the ability and strength of the two started doubts, but he would give it a try.

After a trip to show Karl the fields and equipment, it was growing dark. A lantern was lit, and Karl and Anna found their way up the stairs to the attic room. There in the dusk of the evening they saw two beds and a window with a curtain.

"Karl, is it all right? Will we be safe?" Anna whispered.

"*Shatz*, we will just thank the Lord for a roof, for good food, and a plan for tomorrow. No travel. We will work hard." His conversation was interrupted by Dritte jumping on the bed and circling around until he found his comfort spot.

Their laughter could be heard through the floor, and the two older people downstairs stopped their rocking to listen to the almost forgotten but most welcome sound.

Mrs. Oldenburg woke the next morning with the feeling of expectation. She lay for a minute trying to remember just what had happened to give her this new anticipation. The whine of the pup brought her to her feet. *Children!* Her husband, awakened by the movement, said, "What is it, Maria?"

"Listen!" As stealthy footsteps came from the attic, "The children and the pup are already up."

The second meal had even less conversation than the first. While Karl and Anna ate, they wondered what this day would hold, but as soon as the last mouthful was swallowed, Mr. Oldenburg said, "We will go to the far field today with the car to bring in the potatoes. The shed is ready, so we dump them there. Some we will sell; some we will keep for our food."

While Karl worked in the potatoes, Anna found there was work for her in the house. After the meals were cleared away, there was preparation for the next meal, but all was not work. Mrs. Oldenburg, working on a quilt, showed Anna how to cut and piece a block. Even in these times, words were few. The woman, although she would have wanted to know Anna's history, was reluctant to question her. Anna told only that they had come out of East Germany and explained how they'd gotten Dritte and, especially, why he was named Three. Even with the smile on the woman's face, Anna saw the tears well up in her eyes.

After eight days, Farmer Oldenburg called a meeting. He and his wife had many late-night talks, debating whether to take on the responsibility of the two children. How could they do that when they knew so little about them? Should they ask about their past? Would they somehow get them into trouble with the government? Yes, they were good workers, and now with good meals and safe rest they were flourishing, and certainly, as Karl had said, they were proving they were strong.

But two children? The debate continued as they wrestled with the problem of some sort of education if they stayed.

Then there was the simple problem of noise in the house. It had grown very quiet since *the boy* had left for the army, and they had accepted that as normal. Did they want their normal disrupted? No, these two were not very noisy. Even the pup used his energy outdoors. Yes, they reluctantly admitted, with few words, they *did* like to hear the young voices and occasional laughter.

Yes? No?

What if the children didn't want to stay? How long would they stay?

At the end of the eight days, Mr. and Mrs. Oldenburg came to a conclusion.

The farmer, satisfied with the boy's work, and the boy, satisfied with the nearness of his goal city, reached an agreement that provided the two children with their dog—and a home.

In the end, it was the promise of school that convinced Karl and Anna to stay. The man not only kept his pledge but encouraged the two, so when the time of grade-school testing came, they each in turn qualified for an upper grade. Long hours at school and their share of farm work filled the next years, until one day it was time for Karl to leave for university. For Anna the separation would have been unbearable except for Karl's confident assurance that when she finished local school she would transfer to the university and join him.

The wind was howling around the corner of the house when Anna laid her pencil in the crease of her book and raised her eyes to look at the flame in the lamp. Many months had passed since Karl moved to the city, and at times the loneliness nearly smothered her. If Mrs. Oldenburg had been just a little ... a little *what*? She was kind, not cross, and a friendly companion, but even if only Anna had been able to call her something other than Mrs. Oldenburg. Aunt maybe, or even grandmother—something less rigid.

Anna's thoughts were interrupted by the scrape of Mr. Oldenburg's chair. This was the signal it was time to end the day. He walked to the tiny parlor and, opening the door, crossed to the table where the Bible was kept. This was one part of the day Anna had grown to love. In the orphanage, when the Bible was read, she'd struggled to understand, but now, years later, that had changed. It had happened one night just days before Karl left for the city. That night, Mr. Oldenburg had begun his reading with Psalm 23, and from there, without comment, he'd turned to John 10 and read about the Good Shepherd.

Karl and Anna listened, drinking in each word. They had known someone was taking care of them as they'd traveled and, remembering the Christiansens' and Elsie's faith, had concluded there was someone somewhere. But that night they'd met the One who cares. They understood that God had sent His Son to be the faithful, loving Shepherd and they could be among His sheep.

When the lamps had been turned down and the house was quiet, Anna had said, "Karl, I believe Jesus is my Shepherd."

"Me too," Karl replied.

"Remember when Elsie would tell us we could trust Jesus as our Savior?" Anna asked. And before Karl could answer, she continued, "I believe God and trust Jesus as my Savior."

"Me too!" Karl called from behind the cloth wall that separated them.

That night, as Mr. Oldenburg read his Psalm and the New Testament chapter, Anna listened with appreciation and gratitude. She had no father or mother but a gentle, loving Shepherd who would take care of all she needed. She had accepted the Oldenburgs as God's blessing for this time in their lives, and later, snuggling close to Dritte, she prayed: "Thank you, Shepherd God!"

Ties to the potato farm or its phlegmatic owner had never been strong, so it was not too difficult when Karl, and later Anna, left this home for the final time. Two years had passed since Karl had left for Frankfort, and now it was Anna's time to leave.

"Put your bag here, Anna, and let's tell the Oldenburgs goodbye," Karl said as he deposited the rest of her belongings at the rear of the borrowed car. The older couple had been waiting for them in the kitchen, and as Karl had anticipated, it was not an emotional farewell. The two women embraced and then stood apart while Herr Oldenburg shook Karl's hand and warned, "Work hard."

"Thank you for all you've done for us. We will never forget your kindness," Anna said. She wanted them to know their gratitude was deep and genuine.

"Ja, ja," the woman answered and patted Anna's arm.

Karl, knowing the goodbyes were finished said, "Before we leave, we'll walk out to the shed for a minute."

It was Herr Oldenburg's turn to say "Ja, ja."

The tears that could hadn't come in the past minute now spilled over and ran down Anna's cheeks as she and Karl stood hand in hand beside the small grave behind the little barn.

"Did he go easy?" Karl asked.

"He laid his head on my lap, and I rubbed his floppy ears. He whined and licked my hand, and it was over," Anna explained through her tears. She choked on the words, and Karl pulled her to him and pressed her head against his shoulder. The little animal had been the third member of their family for the growing-up years, and each knew this death signaled the end of that part of their lives.

When Anna could speak, she said, "God knows I do not mean to be irreverent, but wasn't he a gift from heaven when we—I mean, when *I*—needed a sign that we would find safety and a home?"

"You were right the first time. *We,* you and I, needed to know we weren't alone, and God gave us a dog. I don't suppose we'll ever know who left the bread and gave us the pup, but I hope somehow they know how grateful we are ... God knows."

Through a watery smile, Anna whispered, "Goodbye, Dritte."

The next two years were full of change, maturation, and courageous choices for the two of them.

Karl was finishing his last year at university when opportunity came for him and Anna to finish their studies in America. They questioned the possibilities, and friends challenged their judgment, but it was the same daring spirit that brought them to West Germany that finally determined their decision to go to the United States. God had taken care of them for years, and they didn't expect He would desert them if they left Germany. This time the farewells were tearful and reluctant. Karl wondered if Anna had tucked away somewhere in a pocket some sort of reserve against the unknown.

The least painful adjustment was campus to university campus. They learned to say, "Hi" and "How ya doin'?" Except for their accent, they spoke English like natives.

"Thankful for all those hours in language class?" Karl teased Anna as she finished a conversation with a handsome upperclassman.

"Yes, sir!" She grinned.

Their peers dubbed them the "odd couple," for although it was obvious there was no romantic link, there was a strong bond of compatibility and empathy. When Karl's graduation came and he moved to the mountains, their time for each other was limited to Saturdays.

The winter was nearly over, and the day was clear and warm. *Maybe,* he thought later, *that was why we'd had the courage to go into the Mercedes showroom. The weather had inspired an attitude that all was well in the world.*

Rubbing her hand over the top of the white leather on the car seat, Anna said in English, "It is only a dream for us, *ja*, friend?"

"Probably," he replied in German, "but it is a very nice dream, and remember, we've had some mighty good wishes come true."

A man standing at the showroom window listened to the exchange. Their desire to own a Mercedes didn't interest him as much as their easy conversation in the two languages. What an asset someone with that language ability would be! It would be probable, he reasoned, that since they spoke so well they also would read and write English and German. He listened a while longer and then, turning to them, said in German, *"Guten tag!"*

Karl and Anna replied with a smiling *"Guten tag."*

"Do you like the car?" he asked in English.

"Ja," Karl replied.

"And you, Fraulein, do you like the car?" he asked.

Anna patted the silver hood and said, "Yes, very much."

"May I introduce myself? My name is Ean Roberts—and you are?"

Karl extended his hand and said, "This is Anna Klein, and I am Karl Mann."

Mr. Roberts, explaining he was the owner of the dealership, said, "Pardon my eavesdropping, but I was enjoying your use of the two languages, and I appreciated your comment about the car. Are you interested in an automobile?"

"No, as you say, we were ... *admiring*," Karl replied.

"I see ... just as *I* was admiring your fluent exchange. I'll confess, I am interested in your use of both languages. My reason is I often have conversations and correspondence in German, and since I'm not good at either speaking or writing German, I am looking for someone who is comfortable in both languages. This person would work as an assistant to me. Are either of you looking for a job?"

Karl looked from the speaker to Anna and said with a grin, "You see? Our dream is coming true already." But with the determination of one who knows where he's going and no intention of changing, said to Mr. Roberts, "Thank you for the offer, but my future is in writing editorials, not car contracts."

Without hesitating, Roberts turned to Anna, "How is it with you, Anna? Are you going to write editorials too?"

"No, my field is business," she informed him.

"Business and language—that's a remarkable combination. Could I interest you in looking over a position here?" he asked.

"Probably not. I'm still at the university and have some months before I graduate."

This information didn't deter but seemed to inspire the dealer, so that before Karl and Anna left the showroom it was settled that she would come in after classes on Monday to talk over a work arrangement.

By evening Karl was counting the minutes until he could take Anna to her dorm. The rest of the afternoon he had listened to excited prattle about new clothes, an apartment of her own, a checking account with Anna Klein printed on each check, and most wonderful—a car. Not that he wasn't pleased to see her happiness or that he didn't share in her excitement, but he admitted to himself, here was a part of Anna he'd never seen or maybe just hadn't noticed. The little brown-eyed girl who used to walk or work herself to the point of exhaustion to prove she could keep up with him, the same little girl who, when she had done all she could, would lean on him for support, had taken a giant step without him. This was a revelation he'd have to think about.

Karl took Anna home after dinner. From the restaurant to the campus he'd listened to a wild prophecy of dreams coming true, and when she'd finally closed the car door and run up the walk, a sad loneliness settled on Karl.

Neither knew, but they would soon discover that both dreams and nightmares can be parented by the same beginnings.

Chapter

9

KARL MISSED THE PLEASANT SATURDAYS with Anna, and even when he was meeting her just for dinner, he'd come early to the city.

It was boredom that first drove him to the confines of the city library, but that grew into the challenge to research World War II. He found a peculiar satisfaction in reading opinions and histories about the causes and effects of the conflict. His formative years had been not only influenced but directed by that war, and it seemed every youthful memory was gray, and urgent, and washed over with feelings of fright. He needed to see that time of his life from an adult perspective.

The second Saturday without Anna, Karl's errands were finished by midday, so began his research in the library's history division. The room was quiet and deserted, except for one lone figure who sat bent over a clutter of books and papers. Several hours had passed when Karl looked up from his collection of journals and commentaries to see the other table still occupied. This time he noticed the one studying was a very attractive young woman. What would keep a pretty girl for these long hours? he wondered. He needed to stretch, and hoping not to make too damaging an interruption, he walked to the other table and whispered, "Excuse me."

She looked up and responded with a pleasant hello. He was surprised he had not startled her. He offered an apology for disturbing her studies but said he needed a rest and wondered if she would join him. She pushed her chair back and, with a small nod, followed him out to the wide concrete front steps.

Karl said, "My name is Karl Mann, and I'm doing some research on the massive subject of World War II. You look immersed in some subject too."

She nodded and said, "I'm Lisal Schiller, and I, too, am studying the war. It is a large subject, is it not?"

For some reason, Karl felt he must be cautious when he answered. He hesitated., " I have some personal reasons for my quest, so that keeps me in the books." Not wanting to reveal any more than he already had, he said, "Then too, I am a journalist, so research of any kind will sometimes prove useful. Are you studying for pleasure, or do you have some academic reason?"

He listened to her vague reply and watched her gray-blue eyes. Suddenly, he was aware of the sound of her voice. She had a Deutsche accent! A little grin pulled at the corners of his mouth, and as soon as she'd finished her sentence, he frankly asked, "Are you German?"

A spark of resistance flashed in her eyes but quickly died. She perceptibly relaxed and answered, *"Ja."*

Turning away from him, she said, "I'd better finish my project for today. Another time, perhaps?" And she walked into the building.

Karl followed, and in that prescribed quiet of the library once again, he looked down at his books. Minutes passed, but he knew his concentration was over for the afternoon, so stuffing his papers into his folder and shelving the books, he returned to the tables. Lisal had disappeared.

Chapter

10

LISAL'S QUICK GLANCE TOLD HER Karl Mann was still at his table. She gathered her folders and walked out into the Colorado sunshine. The late-afternoon sun shone on the bright gold of the capitol dome, and the sidewalk was crowded with shoppers and workers hurrying home. Usually she felt a thrill being part of the life of the city, but today her mind was occupied with replaying this afternoon's meeting and short conversation.

So many questions! Why do I feel like I should have some connection with this man? How did this German fellow come to be in the United States? Could I have met him before? Quite unlikely, and yet ... yet there was that strange sensation of knowing him. A few more steps and more pleasant thoughts pushed aside the questions. He is handsome! And polite! He has a job he obviously enjoys. He said he wanted to research the war to satisfy his curiosity. He is very good looking ... and so tall! Lisal realized she was smiling. *I feel like a school girl*, she thought, *but he is ... well ... attractive!*

Since leaving school the opportunities to meet people her age had been few. She and her father had talked of college, but both were content with their life of travel. How many times had they come to America? Enough so that it was as much home as Germany.

It was too early to return to the hotel, so she turned off Broadway and followed the crowd up the hill. The streets east of Denver, the capitol, were lined with solid, opulent mansions built by some of the ambitious founders of the western movement.

Early in the city's history, Mr. Brown had platted his pastures and fields, and because the area was the high point, the lots became the desirable area to build the sturdy three-storied homes. She had read of those pioneering men and women. Many had come to the wild Colorado prairies with all their possessions in wagons. They had been the visionaries, dreaming of building a new, thriving extension of what they'd left in the East.

Lisal dreamed too as she strolled by the elaborate wrought-iron fences, wide porches, sparkling beveled-glassed front doors, many with Tiffany stained-glass insets. Driving by at night, one could see the twinkling crystal chandeliers through partially opened heavy drapes.

Her own lifestyle was comfortable, but the elegance that radiated from these houses stirred her curiosity. Even as she tried to picture how it would feel climbing the broad staircases, her thoughts turned back to the present. She had much to be thankful for. Her own history could have been much different—it could have ended when she was just a child.

As always, with these thoughts she felt a shiver. But now, this afternoon, she chose not to allow the past to shadow the bright day.

Her steps had been steady and strong as she walked block after block. Finally, turning back down the hill, she moved toward the hotel. Hardly realizing it, Lisal smiled at those she passed, and they—appreciating a friendly face—returned the smiles.

Only one block to go, and she slowed her pace. By now the smile had changed to a grimace as the old wound reminded her she'd walked too far.

Chapter

11

Disappointed but not surprised, Karl gathered his things and wandered out to his car. Pretty girl, he thought, and nice too. Great eyes—something special about those eyes.

He maneuvered the car through Saturday-afternoon traffic and parked a block from Anna's work so he could enjoy a leisurely walk.

The wide windows of the dealership reflected the late-day sun, and the insignia of gold on the door glistened in the bright rays. Karl sat on one of the upholstered sofas in the showroom and watched the lingering clients. The tasteful design on the area, the classic cars, and the people gave the room an attitude of assured sophistication. Anna fit right in. She sat at her desk: alert, attractive, and confident. "This evening," Karl mused, "I'll tell her how good she looks." He watched as she cleared her desk and carried some files to Mr. Roberts's office.

"Gute nacht, Herr Roberts," she said.

When he replied, "Gute nacht, Fraulein Anna," she grinned at his achievement.

"Your German is improving, sir," she said, encouraging him.

"Thanks to you, young lady. Have a good weekend, and we'll see you Monday."

Karl pulled Anna's arm through his as they walked to his car. The sound of the regular click of her high heels on the pavement and a sideward glance at the slight tilt of her chin brought Karl's eyebrows up. *What happened to the kid?* When had his determined little crusty marshmallow gone away and in her place come this lovely young woman?

"Anna, if you don't beat all."

"What?" She looked at him in surprise. "What in the world are you talking about, and where did you get that expression?" She was laughing at him now.

"Wall, pardner, I think I got it from some dad-burned cowboy movie, and what I mean is you're just about the purtiest little filly around!" Karl chuckled.

"Karl!" Anna's face glowed with appreciation.

"I mean it, Anna. You look great at your desk, and you are pretty."

"Well, friend, I'll tell you; you're not so bad yourself. Any girl would be pleased to be walking next to you."

Through dinner they reveled in this newfound appreciation for each other, and the banter continued. Across a last cup of coffee, Anna began telling Karl about her week.

"Mr. Roberts introduces me to every client and salesman. We ..." She was embarrassed using the plural term, but continued, "We make it a point to be acquainted with each person who comes in. This is a goal for me, since he calls each person by name and asks that I do the same. Wednesday I met a ..." She paused, searching for the right word, "disquieting man. He's a salesman. That's not unusual, of course, but what seems strange is that, although he is German, he speaks with a definite English accent. And there is his almost-too-perfect American name."

"Well?" Karl questioned. "What's his so called American name—John Smith?"

Her eyes widened, and she opened her mouth as if to respond, but then she laughed. It started out as a giggle, but as if there was some hilarious joke, she was soon laughing until the tears trickled down her cheeks. Karl's puzzled gaze brought her back to the conversation as he asked, "What is so funny about the name John Smith?"

To Karl's surprise the humor left her eyes, and in its place rested a shadow of fear, the look that once had been so at home there.

"It isn't the name that is funny. It is that you should have guessed it, and that to you it seems so inconsequential. Sorry I lost control, but when I met John Smith, I had the strangest feeling. It lasted just a speck of time, but the memory of it will not go away."

Concerned, Karl asked, "Was he threatening or what?"

"No, nothing like that. He is a very handsome gentleman. His voice is quiet and his smile pleasant. I don't understand my reaction either, but I feel some relief just telling you about him."

Karl persisted. "How do you know he's German, since he speaks with an English accent?"

"Mr. Roberts told me. He said Mr. Smith is one of his best contacts, because he knows so much about the German market. I don't know, Karl; maybe it's only my imagination. I'll let you know how it goes next time, because he'll be in again the first of next week."

Their conversation shifted to Anna's graduation and the celebration for it. They decided Jon and Kirstin should be invited as well as Mr. Roberts.

Karl leaned across the table and laid his hand on hers. "Anna, my graduation, and now yours, are like landmarks or historical markers that show desperate circumstances are not unbeatable. There are many people, all the way back to Mrs. Jansen and the Christiansens, bless their dear memory, who get credit for helping us get where we are. We've worked hard and steadily to reach our goals. Has not our good God blessed us?" He paused and then said, "Let's celebrate!"

Moisture gathered in her eyes as she nodded her head and smiled.

"Karl, you are a dear," she murmured.

He thought of telling her about the girl at the library but decided against it. Anna needed his full attention and concern tonight. He'd save that bit of information for another time.

Chapter

12

ON MONDAY MORNING, THE TYPEWRITER keys were silent. Thoughts
were stirring around in Karl's mind, but he couldn't get them in
order. The column's first sentence should be catchy or informative,
but none of the first hour's work was right. The subject was there,
but he couldn't hold it still long enough to begin writing about it.
He leaned back in the chair and worried: "What is the problem?"
He loved his work and had great satisfaction in knowing the words
he put on paper caused at least some people to think and respond
to the issues raised. That challenge was usually all the stimulation
he needed, but this morning even that objective could not control
his wandering mind. His finger tapped out an uneven rhythm on
the arm of the chair, and his eyes stared, unseeing. He'd relax for a
minute and let his brain clear.

He drew his feet from under the desk and stood, turning his
back to his work. The coffee was still hot, so he filled his cup and
looked down into the brown liquid. There his gaze held, as if staring
into a crystal ball. Instead of relaxing, he felt a knot grow in the pit
of his stomach. For the first time that morning, his thoughts began
to take shape, but they were not ideas for a *Timberline* editorial. No,
he was remembering part of Saturday's conversation with Anna. It
was the man, the salesman who had introduced himself to Anna,
that was troubling his thoughts. What could there have been about
a soft-spoken gentleman that would make the girl afraid? For some
reason, she had felt fear when she met him and again when she

relayed the moment to him. But it was more than fear—it was terror! The scene played over and over in his memory. What could be intimidating about a salesman? Whatever the cause, Anna was frightened—and the truth was, her reaction scared him.

For the last few years, life had been good, and he felt an unwelcome twinge of resentment that any shadow of a childhood fear could resurrect fright in him. Surely it was their unique relationship that raised this empathy. Surely! Everyone has times of alarm, and Anna had blown the incident way out of proportion. He'd call tonight and assure her, and himself, that the John Smith incident was a passing specter, and everything was okay.

With that resolve, he put a fresh paper in his typewriter and settled his mind to work. Later, when he was satisfied with his copy, he locked the office and started home.

Winter was hard on the dirt roads in the mountains, and the short lane to the house was so deeply rutted he had to shift down to get the car up the slight incline and into his parking place.

Even though it was May, small patches of snow lay in the shady sides of rocks and trees, and where the sun had melted it, the pinkish-white pasque flower shyly announced the approach of summer. Seeing the blossom reminded Karl of Kristin's story about the race she and Jon had going. Each spring they challenged one another to see who would find the first pasque flower, and the winner won a dollar. He smiled as he thought of the race and the prize. Those two had a way of taking an ordinary incident and turning it into an event of their own. *Good friends they are*, he mused, *and great examples of marital contentment.* The commitment they shared had become his motivation to wait for a woman with whom he could share that same quality of life. "Two becoming one"—what a rapturous goal. Rapturous? What little speck of his gray matter harbored amorous words like that? He grinned to himself. *Old Bigelow would shake his shaggy head if he knew I had such a romantic cache. I'm a little surprised myself!*

Leaning against the fender of the car, his eyes searched out other sunny spots for the flower.

"Karl, are you going to stand outside forever?" a voice called from the kitchen door.

He could hear the smile in her voice, and that brought a smile in return. Coming in and pushing the house door shut with his foot, he laid a tattered file folder on the counter. There, on a purposely swept-clean area, and in a pretentious vase, waited the modest little blossom. Kirstin would be a dollar richer.

"Anna called this afternoon and asked that you call her tonight," Kirstin said.

"I'd intended to call her anyway. Did she say what she wanted?" Karl asked.

Frowning, Kirstin said, "No, not exactly. She must have been at her desk, because I got the impression that she didn't want to say too much. She murmured a name, and I thought she said John Smith, but I suppose I misunderstood. She seemed apprehensive and quite emphatic that you should call."

The smile faded from Karl's face, and the comfortable thoughts of the last minutes vanished. Kirstin watched his eyes narrow and a frown spread across her forehead.

"Job problems?" Kirstin asked.

"I'm not sure. You weren't mistaken about the name, and you may have been right guessing she sounded urgent. To tell you the truth, I've been bothered about this John Smith ever since the conversation I had with her Saturday night." He told her about Anna's laughter and tears and her fear.

He called, but no one answered in Anna's dorm room, so he put the receiver in the cradle and walked to his room, where he sat on the edge of the bed.

"What's happening, God? This fear of Anna's is like a cold—she caught it, and now I've got it. I'm not a child anymore, I'm a man, but I have this absurd, unnecessary aggravation. It's making me feel defensive—but defensive against what? Against a man with a common American name, or is it self-protection because I don't want to face the old enemy, fear?

"For Pete's sake!" he muttered out loud. He stood up, thrusting his hands deep in his pockets. "Why am I so shook up? Anna could have been having a bad day. We don't even know the man, and if we did—or if Anna did—what could she have done, or he have done, to make her afraid of him? Our lives since the orphanage have been relatively commonplace. At least our relationship with other people has been strictly ordinary."

He took a mental inventory and could find no significant person or event that would have the power to make the stable Anna panic. Who then was John Smith?

With every sense he wanted to deny it, but the premonition of danger was real. From somewhere, either from without or within, came a warning. It was not a clear call but an undefined urge to be prepared.

Kristen's, "Hello?" made him realize the phone had rung.

"Karl, it's Anna," she called.

He had seconds to buck up. Into the receiver he said, "Hi!"

Before he could continue, Anna's strained voice said, "Karl, he was here again today, and he asked question after question. It wasn't an interrogation, because he made it like a conversation, but he asked about my past. He wanted to know where I was born, who my parents were—"

"Whoa!" Karl interrupted. "Let's do this a little slower." Cautiously, he asked, "It's Smith you're talking about, right? What's so unusual about asking someone about one's background? Maybe he was just making conversation."

"No! I mean, at first it was small talk, but his questions became more specific, and I began to feel my answers were extremely important to him. Karl," There was a sob in her voice. His hand tightened around the receiver. "I told Mr. Smith the truth. I said I knew I'd been born in Germany but didn't know where and that my parents had been killed in the war. Then he sympathized with me and said he supposed I'd been raised by relatives. I was so foolish—"

No more words came. The line was silent except for the sounds of ragged breathing. Karl knew Anna was weeping.

He wanted to sympathize, to tell her everything would be all right and not to worry, but instead his voice lost the casual façade, and he snapped, "What difference does it make what you answered!"

Even thought he was surrounded by the pleasant walls of home, there was a sharp picture in his mind of two vulnerable children, and the untimely memory angered him. He was instantly ashamed of his agitation but lashed out anyway, "Anna!"

Slowly, as if every syllable was wrong from her, she spoke, "I told him I'd lived in an orphanage." Again the line was silent.

"Yes, and ...?"

"And when I said that word ..."

"What word?"

"Orphanage. When I said *orphanage*, I was looking at his face." She stopped again.

"Come on, Anna. You looked at his face, and what?"

It was just a whisper, but he heard each word. "And then I knew." The line was toneless—she was caught up in reliving the scene.

"Anna!" This was not harsh demand but a sort of pleading.

"Karl, I knew that Mr. Smith is the man who came to the orphanage with the men and the guns."

Chapter

13

KIRSTIN HADN'T CONSIDERED IT BAD manners to stand in the hall and listen to Karl and Anna's conversation. She because the strain in Karl's voice alarmed her.

"Who is this John Smith?" she asked when Karl hung up.

Karl's lips barely moved as slowly he said, "He is bad news from the past. He may be the instigator of a brutal tragedy in postwar Germany."

Kirstin was aghast, and she blurted, "How awful! But what could that have to do with Anna?"

"I hope it will have nothing to do with her, but this Smith has revived some memories we would rather forget."

He hedged, "Something about him makes her suspicious, but there is no proof; it may be only a resemblance to the man we knew. After all, in America one is innocent until proven otherwise. Right?"

He paused, but to keep her from questioning further, he continued, "But guilty or not, he won't be in the city indefinitely, because he's a salesman from Germany. Sooner or later he'll have to return home. Sooner, I hope."

She sensed he wanted the conversation ended, so she said no more, but his attempt to smooth it over was betrayed by the stress in his voice and on his face.

For Karl the usual contentment of the mountain home was absent, so early in the evening he excused himself and went to his room. Anna had insisted nothing could be accomplished by a trip to the city, but he wished he'd gone anyway. Maybe talking face to face would make the suspicion less intimidating. It was almost absurd to think the man could enter their lives again. If it was him, what difference could it make, except to make them look back to a time in their childhood they'd rather forget? They could cope with that.

Karl picked up his Bible and read several Psalms. Later he prayed, "David faced threats and even danger, but he steadfastly trusted You, Father. We don't even know this Smith is a threat, but I do know I've given way to fear. Thank You, Father, for the reminder from Your Word that You are fully aware of everything that concerns me and that You're my fortress and strength. I don't know what lies ahead, but God, I commit it to you. Would You give me courage to trust You to work out this situation for me?"

On Saturday, just before noon, Karl walked up the wide steps of the public library. He'd decided to put aside the study of war for the time being, but consider investigating some harmless subject, or better yet he'd investigate the study of girls—one in particular. He doubted any subject would hold his attention while he waited for Anna, but he was hoping to find the same girl he'd met the week before. "It's a paradox. I can't bring myself to open the books on World War II because of one German, but I can't keep away from the library because of another."

She was there. Karl picked up a magazine and joined her at the table. She smiled when he asked, "How are you?"

"Fine, and you?"

They whispered back and forth until Karl asked, "How about lunch?"

Lisal agreed. The downtown café was crowded, and conversation was limited until the waitress cleared a booth and seated them. "The special is German sausage sandwich and fries," she said.

"I'll take a hamburger and Coke, please," Lisal ordered, and

Karl asked for the same. Lisal raised her eyebrows and, grinning, said, "No sauerkraut?"

"*Nein, fraulein.* Burgers for me."

Their easy laughter was followed by talk of favorite foods, and when the waitress set their plates down, Karl, without hesitation, said "Let's pray."

Lisal bowed her head, but Karl realized he barely knew this girl. Embarrassed by his own assumption, he paused, uncertain what to do. When he and Anna met for dinner, there was never a question whether to stop and thank the Lord for their food—but what would this girl think of the practice? He was staring at the top of her bowed head; if he didn't do something quick, he'd be looking at her face. He began, "Father ..." and while his mouth said all the right words, his heart was praying, "Forgive me for being embarrassed to pray!"

At the amen, Lisal raised her head and began pouring catsup on her hamburger. Karl watched and thought, "She's either a good actress or praying is nothing new. Hope it's the latter."

Through the meal, Karl told her about Jon and Kirstin, their home in the mountains, and the *Timberline.* "What brings you to the city on Saturdays?" she asked.

He replied, "I have a friend here, a special person I've known since childhood, and we spend the evening together. She's finishing at the university and working at Roberts' Mercedes as an interpreter."

"An interpreter at a car dealership? How strange," Lisal remarked.

"It's not as unusual as it seems. Mr. Roberts, her boss, needed a bilingual person to take up where his German failed, and Anna, my friend, can do the job. She thinks the work is challenging and mostly enjoyable."

Lisal raised her eyebrows, and leaning her elbows on the table asked, "Mostly enjoyable? It is sometimes unpleasant?"

He looked at her, trying to decide whether to tell anything about Smith. It was not after all, a concern of this girl's.

"Is the work sometimes too demanding" Lisal persisted.

Karl decided. "No, Anna likes the demands and the variety. The fly in the ointment, so to speak, is that she's having a little problem with one of the salesmen. Incidentally, the man is a German who speaks with an English accent, and his name is John Smith."

If he expected Lisal to see any humor in the description, he was disappointed. For several seconds she sat unmoving, and finally she let out a brief, "Oh?"

Unmindful of her reaction, Karl went on. "It's a complicated situation, but we know this man won't stay in America indefinitely. We're hoping he leaves soon. Very soon."

"We? Both you and Anna are hoping he leaves? The wish is not just Anna's?"

"No, not at all. Remember I told you I had a personal reason for reading about World War II? I'm trying to see that time from a more objective perspective, because my memories are through the eyes of a child and are pretty bleak. All those years were tough, but there was one … incident that was personally tragic, and it's this Smith who reminds us of that time."

He searched her face as he tried to explain. Finally he said, "That's enough. This is far too involved and no doubt sounds like a mystery to you. Let's end the subject. Tell me about yourself. Do you live in the States now?"

Lisal told him she was temporarily in the city with her father, and while he attended to his business, she was free to sightsee and shop. Since there was only the two of them, she traveled with him. When she described her home on a German river, Karl shared his memories of boating on the same waterway. They discovered each could describe the same castle on the bluff overlooking the river. Pleasant hours passed. Reluctantly Karl said, "I need to leave and meet Anna. I'll walk you to the library. Could I see you next week?

I'm coming to the city on Wednesday. Would you have dinner with me?"

Lisal smiled and said, "I'd like that. We, my father and I, are at the Brown Palace."

Plans were made, and as she climbed the steps to the library, Karl drove off to the car dealership.

Karl took Anna's hand as they left Robert's. He asked, "How did it go today? Did you see Smith?"

"He hasn't been in since Wednesday. I've noticed a pattern. He'll come to the dealership on Tuesday or Wednesday, or as he did this week, three days, but we won't see him the rest of the week. I think he goes to another city. I'm sure of it."

"What makes you think he is out of town?" Karl asked.

"Because of how he phrased his invitation to you and me for dinner next Wednesday evening." There was a tremor in her voice. She was relieved they had reached the car and could sit in its privacy.

"What do you mean, Anna, that he included me in the invitation?"

Immediately he was ashamed of what his question implied. "I'm sorry. I didn't mean it the way it sounded. What I want to know is why he is inviting you, or both of us, to dinner. Does he realize your feelings toward him or that you might suspect he was one of the men at the orphanage?"

"I don't know if he noticed my reaction, but I know this: he is one of those men. He is the one who did the talking. I realize it was more than ten years ago, and I know I was just a child, but when I said the word *orphanage*, I was looking at his eyes, and I knew he was the same man. There was an instant recognition, and Karl, at that moment I think he suspected who I might be. Do you want to know how it came about that you were included in the invitation? He is so devious. Just his presence makes me fear and despise him! I question every word he says and every move he makes, because everything about him seems to have some hidden motive."

"Does Mr. Roberts seem to have doubts about the man?" asked Karl.

"No, the two are great friends. They've done business for several years and seem to have the highest regard for each other," Anna replied.

"Could you be wrong about him, Anna? Do you think there is simply a resemblance between the salesman and the man at the orphanage? It's been a long time." Karl said trying to rationalize.

"I've gone over and over every memory and compared what I remembered with what I'm seeing and feeling. It isn't as if I can recall exactly what he looked like—that's lost. But it's his voice and the look in his eyes that match perfectly with what is forever marked on my memory. I am positive he is the man who did the talking and ordered the execution," she insisted.

The two sat in silence. When Karl spoke, he said, "How did he ask you to bring me to dinner?"

"Oh, yes. He said if I had a friend I should bring him along. He could be wondering if it is possible that the two of us are still together. He is getting answers without asking questions! I am afraid of him, Karl."

Karl's expression was thoughtful, and he nodded his head. Leaning forward, he said, "We might have reason to be scared, but Anna, God is not going to abandon us to Mr. Smith or to whatever Mr. Smith may have decided about us. The Lord is aware of whatever the man is thinking or whatever he may be planning."

The two friends were quiet over their last, lingering cup of coffee. The restaurant noise was abating after the dinner rush, and here and there others talked and laughed in subdued tones. In the pleasant dimness of the dining room, Karl looked across the table at Anna, but he wasn't seeing her. His mind was busy examining what they knew of John Smith and Anna's frightened reaction to him. *Steady and calm, that's this girl—and straightforward. If she looked at this man and is convinced of his identity, I must believe her. From now on we'll assume we know who Smith is. How he came to be a car salesman* or happened across our path is a question to solve later. *The immediate issue is how to stay out of his way. Even though the man did not pull the trigger, he was a killer then, and he may be one now.*

We could go to the police. If we told them all about Smith—but would American policemen believe a story from childhood memories that happened years ago in Germany? Why should they? We couldn't offer them one shred of proof. There's probably no hope of help from that source. Maybe there isn't anyone who can help, but one thing is sure—we won't run. For years all we did was run, and hide, and cower. We will not go back to skulking. His jaw hardened, and the paper napkin crackled as he crushed it into a tight ball.

As if his companion had read his thoughts, she said, "I think we should face him."

A slow blink brought the surroundings and Anna's comment into focus. Their eyes met and held. *This is one gutsy girl.* He didn't say aloud what he was thinking but instead said, "You're right."

Tossing the crumpled paper onto a plate, he said, "Let's find out about this guy. This time, we'll be the ones asking the questions. He can tell us where he was during the war and postwar years, and if we get the answers we suspect, we'll confront him with the day at the farm. The witnesses the man left may have to speak again. Tell him you do have a friend you'd like to bring to dinner."

Her fingers tightened on Karl's arm, and she said, "It sounds so easy to do, but I know I'll be scared to death to face him with these questions."

"You aren't alone there. But remember Mrs. Jansen's favorite verse, the one we'd hear regularly? 'My help comes from the Lord.' He'll help us; He promised."

Anna withdrew her hand. Folding her two hands together, she rested them on the cleared table and leaned forward to look Karl full in the face. "Yes, Karl, I remember," she said deliberately, "but I also remember Mr. Smith shot Mrs. Jansen."

Chapter

14

TRUE TO ROUTINE OF THE past weeks, the salesman appeared Monday morning.

"Good morning, my dear."

Anna hoped the thin smile didn't look wholly artificial as she responded, "Good morning, Mr. Smith."

Seated in the bright showroom and surrounded by people, her fears could stay at bay for the moment. She could struggle to masquerade her feelings if he didn't stay standing there or try to carry on more conversation. He broke into her resolve with, "I would like to confirm our dinner reservations for Wednesday night. Did you find a friend to bring with you?"

"Yes," she replied.

Mr. Smith agreed with the plan that she and the other guest would meet him at the restaurant.

"Your friend has a car?" he asked.

"Yes."

"Then he will pick you up?" he inquired.

Why the questioning? Anna looked down at her desk and began to sort papers. She murmured a yes and desperately hoped he would think he was interfering with her work. She could feel him hesitate and then walk away. She let out her breath. *He makes me think of a hunter tormenting his prey, and Karl and I are his prey. He knows who my friend is, and he's getting morbid enjoyment hoping we know who he is. He feels so safe.*

"Oh, God, are You there?"

When Karl called, Anna explained, "He's made reservations for seven, and I told him we'd meet at the restaurant. Don't think I'm being dramatic about the situation, but honestly, sometimes when I think about it, I feel we are actors in some melodrama."

"I know what you mean, Anna, but at the same time, be careful. I don't know how we'll go at this on Wednesday, but there won't be any playacting, I'm convinced. Every line will be real."

He explained he wouldn't be picking her up, but meet him early at the restaurant, so they could have some time together before they faced Smith.

Without questioning his plan, Anna agreed. When he hung up, he admitted he had again, on purpose, failed to tell Anna about Lisal. Not the right time, he convinced himself.

It was 5:50 Wednesday when Karl called for Lisal, and straight away apologized that the evening would be cut short. Briefly he told her about dinner with John Smith. She seemed satisfied with his explanation and teasingly said, "Let's go for a drive, since you can't hang around long enough for dinner."

He turned the car as if to go to the mountains, but Lisal said, "Do you know the park with the Parthenon-like building?" He shook his head.

"Why, Karl, haven't you investigated every inch of this beautiful city? Where is your reporter's curious nose? You should know all the interesting spots by now. I could take you to nearly every museum or art gallery, and I think I've visited all the shops. I do have to admit I look at this place with tourist's eyes you see it as home. Maybe," she admonished with a twinkle, "you take for granted all it has to offer."

She directed him to the park's entrance, and as they turned into its winding lanes, the landmark clock on the grassy island struck six.

"Don't worry. It's always a little fast," Lisal assured him as he checked his watch.

"Do you come here often?" Karl asked.

"As often as I can. Did you see the bike rental near the gate? I catch a streetcar from the hotel to that corner, rent a bicycle, and explore this lovely place. Since you haven't been here before, you wouldn't know about the lookout tower. Shall we go there and climb it?"

"Sorry I'm so unacquainted! You show the way, and we'll go climb a tower!" he replied.

"Good! There is a spectacular view from the top. It takes in the city and the mountains, and if you turn east you can see for miles out across the prairies."

Lisal directed Karl, and as a light rain began, they pulled into the parking lot. The tall metal tower poked up through the mist, and Karl could see people standing on the graduated landings.

"Let's go to the second level," Lisal said, "where we can at least see over the treetops."

As they started up the corrugated steps, Karl took her hand. He was pleased she didn't pull away but instead folded her fingers around his and smiled at him.

Grinning back, he said, "Watch your step, Fraulein, the wet has made these steps slick."

Lisal told Karl how she often stood at the top of the tower looking from landmark to landmark, and by that process discovered where her hotel stood and where the major streets cut across the city.

"There, just to the left of the Civic Center spire, is the street you'll take to the Black Forest Inn. Do you see it?" she asked.

Instinctively he looked at his watch before he followed her pointing finger. 6:15. They'd have to leave. He would just have time to drop off Lisal at her hotel and get to the Inn by 6:50.

"Yes, I can see it, and I wish I could take one giant step and be there, but since I have to go the conventional way, we'd better be going. I am sorrier than you know that I must leave you and go to this dinner."

Descending, Lisal was answering his question about her length of stay in the city when she slipped. Karl half turned to catch her, but the rain-slick rail and steps put him off balance, and when he grabbed her she slipped under his arm and bounced down the stairs. Helplessly he watched her come to rest on the landing. She was conscious when he reached her.

"Don't touch me. Just let me be," she whispered.

He knelt beside her. "Are you badly hurt? Do you think anything is broken? Can you use my jacket for a pillow?"

His jumbled effort to be helpful brought a small smile as she repeated, "Just let me rest for a minute. I'm not hurt except for my ankle. I think it may be broken."

Karl patted her hand and waited for the first pain to pass. Finally, she asked, "Would you help me sit up and lean against the rail, please?"

He raised her, and as she scooted back to the metal slats, several people gathered and offered help.

"We think it's her ankle," Karl said, "but we need to wait a bit longer before she can be moved. When she feels able, if someone would support her on the other side, I think we could get her down from this landing and to my car."

Lisal looked at her watch and said, "If we could wait just a few more minutes."

Karl was aware of the time—6:45. He wouldn't leave Lisal to strangers—yet how could he abandon Anna?

Finally Lisal said, "I think I can move, Karl. Please go slow with me, and I'll make it to the car."

With every faltering step Karl felt the minutes ticking by. As soon as he could get Lisal to an emergency room, he'd call the restaurant and have Anna paged. She could leave and come to where he was. He must not leave her alone with Smith.

Where was a hospital? Lisal said she didn't know. It was after seven when Karl found a gas station and directions. Everything seemed to be moving in slow motion, and several more minutes passed before they were at the hospital and in an examining room.

"I'm sorry I have disrupted your dinner plans. Can you reach Anna, do you think?" Lisal asked.

Karl squeezed her hand and said, "I'm going to call the restaurant now." Without thinking he said, "I hope she is all right."

Lisal looked at Karl and assured him, "She's fine. She is quite all right."

By the time he'd gone the few steps to the telephone, he'd worked up a panic by reviewing the what-ifs. How could Lisal be so sure Anna was safe? What did she know about their trouble? He dialed the number, and a voice answered, "Black Forest Inn."

"I need to have a woman paged. This is an emergency," Karl explained.

"We do not page, sir, but if you will give a description, I will find the lady and bring her to the phone."

Impatiently Karl described Anna. Standing with his head resting against the top of the phone box, he was numb with apprehension. The probabilities raced through his mind, another starting before one was finished. How could he have failed? But he couldn't have left Lisal. Poor Anna. Dear Anna.

"Sir?" the voice said.

"Yes?" Karl snapped.

"I was the lady's waiter, and she has gone," the man said.

"Gone? How could she be gone? It's only eight."

The waiter said, "I'm not sure of the time now, but I know I did seat the lady and a gentleman a little before seven. There were to be three, but the third person did not come. I served them shortly after seven. They ate hurriedly, I thought, and then they left."

Gone! O, Lord, help! Karl questioned, "Do you know where they went? Of course, you wouldn't. Can you tell me this—did she look upset?" he asked, "Did she look frightened?"

"No, sir. Her companion was a distinguished gentleman and was very attentive. As I said, when the third person was late in coming, the two ordered, ate, and left. He had his car brought around and he asked for a taxi for the lady. I did think it was a little strange he left in his car before her taxi came. She gave the desk a message for the third party."

"If you please, what did the message say?"

The waiter read, "Karl, I've gone home."

"Home?"

"That's what the note says, sir," the man affirmed.

Karl hung up the receiver, relieved and puzzled. Was that the truth? Had she just "gone home"? As his mind cleared, he dialed Anna's number. The phone rang several times with no answer. Where was she? The muddled thoughts frustrated him, and then he remembered Lisal.

Lisal wasn't in the small curtained emergency cubicle, but the nurse told him she would return when the x-rays were completed. Waiting, more waiting.

He stood at the window and watched the car lights reflect off the rain-soaked streets. People moved in and out of the hospital doors, and behind him the waiting room was full of conversations, the turning of magazine pages, and whining children. He felt powerless. He was part of all that was happening but unable to change or stop the unfolding of events.

"Oh, God," his lips moved in silent prayer, "I am grateful that You know all that's happening, but Father, I'm having a tough time trusting You for the outcome." He paused and then continued, "Help me to trust You anyway. Please take care of Anna."

As a hand touched his arm, he turned, and a nurse said, "Your friend is back in her room."

Lisal's ankle was sprained. The doctor put a splint on her leg and advised putting only as much pressure on the joint as was comfortable; Karl marveled at her composure. When, with a faint smile, she asked, "Anna's all right?" he felt a bit of resentment at her innocent nonchalance.

"Hopefully," he answered.

"Oh, I'm sure she is fine," Lisal murmured.

Fine? Her naïve attitude angered him.

"I couldn't reach her at the restaurant since she'd already left for her dorm. She didn't answer my call there, so if you don't mind, I'm going to call again before I take you to your hotel." Karl knew he sounded stiff, but when Lisal nodded, he turned on his heel and hurried out.

On the second ring, Anna answered.

"Hello?"

"Anna, are you okay?"

"Karl, where are you? Why didn't you come?"

Briefly he explained his absence. "Anna, I am wretchedly sorry for abandoning you. I called the restaurant, and your waiter said you'd left in a taxi, but that you'd left a message. What happened there? Are you all right?" he repeated.

Her steady reply reassured him. "Mr. Smith was in the lobby when I got there at fifteen to six. He said we should go to a table, and a waiter could bring you when you arrived. I'd told him we were to meet a little before seven, so when you didn't come by a quarter after we ordered our food. The conversation was a little thin, mostly about cars. When it seemed you weren't coming, we finished our meal, he called a taxi for me, and he left immediately. That's it. That's all there was to it."

Karl asked, "No subtle threats? No probing questions about me and my whereabouts? Nothing, Anna? Are you sure?"

"There was absolutely nothing. It was obvious he felt he'd wasted his time, and under other circumstances I'd have been insulted. Can you figure it out? I'm sure his attitude had everything to do with your absence, but he wasn't dropping any clues."

"Do you want me to come by?"

"No, I'm fine, really. Smith has left the city, I'm sure, for wherever it is he goes, and he won't be back until next Monday. I'm paranoid, I know, but there are more mysterious activities in his life than his occupation with you and me," Anna said. " How about the girl you took to the hospital—how is she ?"

"No bones broken. She had a nasty fall, and I was sure we had major injuries, but there was none. Speaking of her, I'd better deliver her to the Brown Palace."

"Brown Palace? Is she a tourist?" Anna asked.

"Not exactly," Karl explained. "Her papa is here on business, and she travels with him. I must go. I'll see you Saturday, Schatz. Call me if you need me for any reason. *Auf Weidersehen.*"

"*Auf Weidersehen.*"

Lisal was waiting in a wheelchair and beginning to feel the effect of the pain shot. Karl's irritation faded. "How do you feel, Lisal?"

"I feel I've had enough adventure for one night. I'll be glad to get to the hotel. Can you take me home now? Anna all right? Home safe and all?" Her words were slow, and she was having difficulty holding a half smile while Karl answered her queries. Once inside the car she leaned against the door frame and closed her eyes. The harsh, wet glow of the street lights dipped in and out of moving car, and when Karl glanced at the pale cheeks and tightly drawn lips he began to sympathize with Lisal's pain. How could he have been so harsh with her? *"Acht!"*

Had the involuntary exclamation disturbed her? She seemed to be asleep. If the sympathizing driver could have read the thoughts of his wounded passenger, his own thoughts would have been questioning, not sympathetic.

Chapter

15

"HOME ALREADY? I THOUGHT YOU'D be late," Kirstin said as Karl came through the door.

"I am late, or maybe I should say I feel like I've had a long evening," Karl replied.

"Oh, boy! That sounds like a boring date. You did have a date, didn't you?" She paused, but her curiosity won, and she asked again, "Did you have a date?"

"Better than that. I had two!"

"Two?"

"In a manner of speaking two, but I missed the second because I was taking the first one to the hospital."

She put her hand on her forehead as if shading her eyes from the sun and scrutinized him. "Hospital? Karl, you live too sedentary a lifestyle for one word of this to be true. Out with it. What have you been up to?"

"It's all true. You see, I had an early date with a girl I met at the library, and at ten to seven I was supposed to meet Anna and Mr. Smith for dinner. But the first girl slipped and fell, and because I was delayed at the hospital, I didn't meet the second girl."

Patting the arm of a chair, Kirstin said, "You'd better sit down and tell me the whole story, and don't leave out a detail. Sounds better than a soapbox opera," she exclaimed.

"Soap opera," he corrected.

"That's what I said."

He wished the day's events had been as simply explained as a soap opera. To please her, he dropped into a chair, stretching his legs full length and draping his arms off the ends of the armrests, stated, "Sedentary, huh? The girl's name is Lisal Schiller. I've met her a couple times at the library, and I had a date with her tonight. Our time together was supposed to have been cut short because I was to meet Anna and the salesman, Smith, for dinner. We, Lisal and I, drove out to City Park and climbed partway up the viewpoint tower. It had started to rain, so the metal steps were slick. When we were almost down, she slipped, slid past my arm, down the stairs, and collapsed on the landing. How is that for dramatic? You look skeptical. I wonder if you still think I'm telling you a tale!"

Kirstin laughed. "No, I believe every word. But what happened then?"

"I thought she had broken a leg or worse. We couldn't move her right away, but with help from some bystanders, we got to the car and finally to a hospital. By then it was after seven, and I was late for the dinner date. That caused me no small anxiety! I was concerned about Anna, but I couldn't leave Lisal."

"Concerned? Because of Mr. Smith?" she asked.

"Yes. I'd promised I'd be with her, because we thought we might confront him with our ..." he paused, "suspicions. But it seems Anna met him, ate without me—and I don't know where Smith went, but Anna went home. They had an uneventful and, according to Anna, boring evening. After I found out she was home, I took Lisal to her hotel, and here I am. Compared to this evening, I'd settle for a sedentary life!"

"I don't know whether to laugh at you or sympathize. I want to hear more about this friend, Lisal, but first, as I remember, you and Anna were pretty shook up by this Mr. Smith. How did a dinner together come about?" she asked.

Karl briefly explained the salesman's invitation to Anna and the request she bring a friend. As he talked, he chose words carefully, but when he finished, Kirstin asked, "Do you really think you need to fear this man?"

Perhaps it was security of the mountain home that encouraged the answer, or maybe it was the need to talk, but whatever the reason, Karl began. "Years ago there was an incident that makes reacquainting with him a possible danger. Anna and I suspect this man is guilty of an atrocity, and actually we think he may be the one who instigated it. The risk is that he may suspect our identities. So, if in fact John Smith is that man, it is possible we are in great danger.

"That's why I went through one hour of torment tonight. I was nearly crazy for Anna's safety, but I felt obligated to see that Lisal was cared for."

Knowing he'd revealed more than enough, Karl changed the direction of the conversation. "We have not come to the end yet, but since Smith leaves the city on Wednesday nights and probably doesn't return until Sunday or Monday morning, we have time to regroup." He emphasized his opinion by quoting, *"Es fließt noch viel wasser den Rhein hinunter."*

"Whatever does that mean? You'll have to translate for me," said Kirstin.

"It's an expression that says, 'Time will go on despite what has just happened,' or literally, 'A lot of water will yet flow down the Rhine,'" Karl explained.

Kirstin responded, "That's a colorful proverb, but how about this one: 'All's well that ends well.'?"

The sound of a car struggling up the rutted drive broke into their exchange. Jon was home. Kirstin met him at the door, and after a kiss and hug, Jon looked past her shoulder and said, "Hey, buddy, what are you doing home? I thought you had an important date."

To answer Jon's query, Karl told him about Lisal's fall and the trip to the hospital. When he told him she had only a twisted ankle, Jon broke in with, "Some original way to end a date," and unwittingly ended Karl's explanation of the evening.

Jon took the coffee Kirstin offered and said, "Mrs. Ryan's baby decided at the last minute to be born C-section, but he is a fine healthy kid. Things were a little harried for a while, but all's well that ends well."

Each, for his own reason, found a measure of comfort in the proverb.

Chapter

16

MR. SMITH'S LEISURELY GAIT AND complacent mask hid the inward, precisely tuned network of problem solving that was at work. A passerby, if he'd noticed him at all, would have smiled at the apparently absentminded handsome man, and as if just catching the pleasantry, Smith would have smiled back. The friendly person on the street would have taken little interest in the strolling gentleman, but John Smith would have observed all. He'd have noted the height, probable age, and clothing and guessed at the nationality in one quick glance. Mostly he would have judged the person's attitude. He counted on the fact that he could anticipate or predict impending actions by analyzing attitude. Rigid self-discipline had taught him always to be aware and to be alert. *Observe and file for future reference*—that was his way of life. More than once this habit had given him the edge on the opposition, and he had never hesitated to make use of every advantage. Suspicion and precaution were brother and sister to him, and he nurtured them as he might have cared for fleshly siblings.

Mr. John Smith sat down on the park bench and carefully laid out the daily paper beside him—that would discourage any talkative visitors. The warm spring afternoon, coupled with the recent irritation, was making him reflective, and he wouldn't welcome conversation with a stranger.

His thoughts traveled from one subject to another, checking and dismissing each idea, until his eyes settled on the passing food vendor. Tamales! His taste ran more to beef steak. Unbidden, an alternative meaning to the name of the cut of meat came to mind. The memory was vivid. At first, many years ago, he hadn't appreciated the term, but when it did not prove harmful, he'd gotten used to being labeled, "beefsteak Nazi." He knew the name-callers meant "brown on the outside but red in the inside." Now, if only he could, he would tell the name-callers that he was once again red all the way through.

When just a boy, his uncle, a man who had risen from simple woodcarver to master cabinetmaker, had advised him to join the Socialist Workers Youth. For the next eight years he'd learned and practiced the tenets of Marxism, but by the mid 30's the young communist realized it would be wise to temporarily leave one youth organization in favor of another, and so gained entrance into the Nazi German Student League. He did not see the changeover as traitorous but as a temporary, unavoidable necessity. The chameleon act had been to his advantage.

Only a select number of university students had been accepted into the League's membership, and in words of Heinrich Himmler, Hitler's second in command, these chosen ones were to serve as the intellectual SS. The Schutzstaffel, or SS, would make good use of those who would go on to be doctors, teachers, lawyers, and other distinguished professionals, for they would be the ones who would spy on their fellow Germans.

The condition that he swear allegiance to the Fuhrer had not been a deterrent, for it had been easy to put on a badge of loyalty when ambition was his true master.

Not only had he, as an intellectual, been welcomed into the SS, but his physical appearance made him highly acceptable. He was tall, blond, and handsome, and to his credit he was free from the taint of Jewish blood for at least the three preceding generations. The Schutzstaffel were, after all, to be the progenitors of Hitler's super race, and the Reich's hatred of Jews made the bloodline a prerequisite.

The one questionable attribute had been the former membership in the communist party, but an unfaltering charade of fierce loyalty removed any doubt of sincerity. He had, during those war years, served them well, and in return the SS had been useful to him. They had used his brains and flawless English to execute their plans, and he had greedily accepted their training to advance his purpose. He became a master of deceit.

No, it hadn't been a problem to have temporarily served as a "beefsteak Nazi," for when the time was right, he had returned to Stalin's party. After a rigid probation period, had been welcomed back to the ranks. But it had not been easy during those trial months when someone watched every action, eavesdropped on every word, and at times seemed to read his very thoughts. Once or twice he'd nearly succumbed to the temptation to lash out at their stupidity, but he'd never yielded. Even when that obnoxious little cell leader had screamed at him for some slight infraction, he had defused the situation by flaunting unworried composure. He'd been confident the party would use him, and he had willingly pledged cooperation and submission. But in the inner man, where even their devices could not reach, there was enshrined that ego which judged and reshaped every assignment in terms of self-profit. Truly he was dedicated to the communist philosophy, but it was he, not they, who would be the master of his fate.

Incredibly, in wartime as now, his was a well-ordered lifestyle— almost as if he was keeping a schedule. The recent, regular trips to America and the weekly Midwestern meetings with his comrades had reinforced that uncluttered routine.

The present crisis would be no more than a temporary out-of-joint link in the strong chain of his habits.

Anna Meier's appearance had been like an echo from the past. But he nodded slightly; there was no danger in echoes. He would find a way to meet, or at least get a look at, her friend, and when the time was right the echo would be silenced. If this man was the boy from the farm, he could be silenced too.

Mr. Smith rested his back against the warmth of the park bench and began evaluation. Anna, he knew, was suspicious of him and yet had accepted the invitation to dinner. She'd consented to bring a friend—that would be the boy.

Smith abruptly crossed his legs, a hint of agitation, over Karl's failure to appear.

Strange he did not come to dinner. He and Anna are comrades, so what would be his reason for neglect? Would he have decided not to attend? Nein. *If he suspects, all the more reason to accompany her—or if he does not suspect, why would he not come? No matter.* Smith uncrossed his long legs.

It is yet possible, he mused, *that Anna has not placed me at the orphanage. She was but a child. If she, or they, do not remember me—all the better. Their identity is certain.* A sly smile crossed his well-groomed face as he felt again that uncanny warning signal that had pulsed through his being when he'd first talked with the girl in the car showroom. He enjoyed a second pleasure as he relived the reminder of his genius. She had obligingly answered his simple questions, and what had started out as a glimmer became a flash, and the connection was made clear. She had recognized something too, for her eyes had betrayed her. *Let her worry about whatever it is she thinks. She is one of the witnesses left at the farm, and it is reasonable this Karl is the other. How regrettable if their presence were to uncover the incident of the past.*

His jaw hardened to a firm line, and he crossed his arms over the muscular chest. Both feet were planted solidly on the sidewalk, and his fierce eyes stared at a colony of ants busily building their fresh pyramid.

Smith had clarified the problem, and one by one he would weigh his options.

If the occasion should arise they would question him, he could deny all allegations or claim party pressure. In his present position as respected car representative, he could claim change of heart and plead remorse—or it would be entirely possible to drop out of sight as unexpectedly as he'd dropped in. A matter of a few hours' office work and he could have a new identity and go to—perhaps—South America. He would know people there as well as here.

The eyelids drooped, and small furrows marred the wide brow. *All of those choices are totally unacceptable. To prevail, one must not take the defensive but the offensive. After all, it is Anna and Karl who are the disrupters, not I. The solution to the problem lies with them. They are not likely to resolve this trouble, so I will have to do it for them. Unfortunate as it is, there is no choice but to remove both possibilities of exposure.*

As if the sun's rays were at work, the frown melted away. Smith stood long enough to grind away the ants' miniature pyramid with his shiny heel, and then he settled once more on the bench. He gathered up his scattered newspapers, clearing the way for someone to sit down. He felt like talking.

Chapter

17

"Karl, who is Lisal?" Anna asked.

It wasn't that he didn't want Anna to know about Lisal, for they had few secrets from each other, but he didn't want her to know how he felt about her. Not yet. The admission of caring, even to himself, threw him off balance, and he groped for words. Fumbling, he answered, "Lisal? She's a girl I met at the library. She's in the States with her papa, and she sprained her ankle."

Anna laughed. "Most of that I could figure out, or I already know. I leave you on your own, and you go right out and find another girl," she teased. "Now tell me something about her I don't know." The candle flickered on the table after their Saturday night dinner.

"Well," began Karl, "she sounds like you when she talks. I mean she has the same German accent with the English. I'm guessing this, but she seems younger than you. Her mother died during the war, so when her father travels, she goes with him. Except for our date at the City Park Tower, all our conversations have been at the library or over lunch. That's where I met her. The library, I mean."

"The library. That's certainly a safe enough place for a meeting." Anna's eyes twinkled. "What is she, a bookworm?"

Ignoring the teasing, Karl went on. "She's been studying World War II; in fact, our first conversation was about our mutual interest. Now you know all," he stated.

"I'm not sure about that, but I'll let you off for now," Anna said, grinning.

Karl looked relieved as Anna changed the subject with, "I found a dress for graduation, and Kirstin sent a note saying they are coming. Mr. Roberts is coming too, and he invited us to his home afterwards. Okay?"

"If that is what you'd like, *Fraulein*, then it's good with me. You and I can celebrate at dinner next Saturday. Wasn't my graduation on a Saturday morning? Wednesday evening seems unusual."

She explained, "There are two ceremonies. The school has divided half the degrees for Wednesday and the rest for Saturday, because there are so many of us. I am to be at the auditorium at 6:30."

"I'll pick you up at six, so you'll be on time and I'll get a good seat."

Karl held the door for her, and as they walked to the car, he said, "Anna, I feel pitifully useless those days Smith is in town and you face him alone. If you need help, would Mr. Roberts be an ally?"

"Mr. Roberts knows, or suspects, nothing, but I am safe in the showroom and office, and I have no need to go beyond those rooms. The man is seldom there past noon and never around when I leave. Be assured, Karl, I am cautious."

As Karl dropped her at the dorm, he wondered how he would feel about leaving her when she'd be alone in an apartment.

Wednesday was overcast, and the weather worsened as Karl drove into the city. "This is a soggy *Springtime in the Rockies*," Karl muttered.

He pulled his car directly in front of Anna's dorm, but before he could open his door, she was running down the walk. He reached over to push the door open, and she slid in, cap and gown in hand. "Karl! He's coming!" she cried.

He shot a glance out the side window, expecting a pursuer, but Anna said, "No! No! Mr. Smith is coming to graduation."

"What? How?" Karl questioned.

"Mr. Roberts stopped me as I was leaving work and asked if I minded if he brought Mr. Smith tonight. He said since we seemed to be friends, and Smith had expressed an interest in attending, he had invited him," she blurted.

Her clasped hands showed white knuckles, and she stared, unseeing, out the window.

Karl sat silent and still, and when he spoke he said, "Anna, I don't believe we have anything to fear at the ceremony. As for after, aren't you sure he always leaves town on Wednesday nights?"

She didn't answer his question but said, "Don't you see, Karl? It's you. He's coming because he knows you'll be there."

The surprise he felt showed clearly on his face. He hadn't expected Smith to come to Anna's graduation, but neither had he reckoned that Smith might not know who he was. When he finally spoke, he said, "If this guy is as convinced of who we are as we think he is, doesn't it seem likely that he already knows who I am? Wouldn't you guess he would have investigated both of us as soon as he suspected? Why does he need to come tonight to see me?"

Anna's voice was raspy. "I don't know. I just thought that might be the reason. Remember how we felt about the man at the farm, that he was cold as ice and heartless?" She paused. "Karl,"—she turned and the words came slowly—"do you think he might be coming tonight so you can see him?"

"What?" His eyes never left Anna's face as he considered the question. "You could be right. It is time I met him and he met me. This should have taken place weeks ago, but whether I've seen him face to face doesn't matter. We are in this together, you and I, and that makes two of us and one of him. When the graduation ceremony is over, we'll stick together. I suppose he'll be at Roberts's afterwards." It was a statement more than a question.

He turned the key, and the engine started. "Stay firm, Schatz, and remember, the One who said He'd never leave us goes to graduations too."

He let Anna out at a side door, and after parking the car he entered the already filling auditorium. It didn't seem likely he'd be able to pick out Roberts and Smith in that sea of faces, but camera ready, he began to search the hundreds of people who were moving through the doors. Karl recognized no one, and when the orchestra began the processional he rose with the crowd. Poor acoustics made it difficult to hear the speeches or the department heads announcing various degrees, so Karl's eyes began to wander from the platform in a methodical row-by-row search for Mr. Roberts and his companion. Without being conspicuous, his view was limited.

He was nearly ready to give up, when involuntarily his eyes darted back over a row, for there had been that flicker of sensation that he'd met someone's gaze. There was Roberts, and the man next to him had to be Smith. It was that eye contact that had drawn Karl back, but now Smith lowered his head so Karl could not see his face. The singular act of having met his gaze pushed, as if for the first time, into the stark reality of danger. It was uncanny that their eyes should have met. Still watching, Karl fussed with the camera, ready to get a quick shot of Smith.

It was not to be. The orchestra was beginning the recessional, and there was no time to lose in following the graduates and finding Anna.

The throng jammed the foyer. Those who did leave let in a rush of cool, wet air that discouraged others from hurrying outside. Look-alike caps and gowns and jostling bodies pushed Karl's frantic search into frenzied urgency. Careful at first, and tense with a grim rudeness, he pushed through the mass toward the door where he'd left Anna earlier. Possibly she would return there. How could he have been so stupid to not plan a meeting place? He chided himself for lack of foresight. He dreaded a face-to-face confrontation with Smith, but in his anxiety to find Anna he made no effort to avoid a chance meeting.

Looking through the collage of faces and backs, he could see there was no Anna at the side door. *Where was she!* How would he find her in this surging mass of people? "Oh God! Help me!"

He turned, and in that instant caught a glimpse of her and a man standing close to the main, middle exit. Pushing and shoving, Karl elbowed his way to the front of the lobby and, leaning hard, he stretched out his hand and grasped Anna's arm.

Startled, she turned and, seeing it was Karl, threw her free arm around his neck. She whispered, "He's gone!"

There was no time for explanation, for Mr. Roberts was speaking to him. "We thought we'd lost you, or I should say Anna was getting so disturbed I was beginning to worry that you had disappeared." Anna grimaced at his idle words. He continued, "You're here now, so let's go on to my place; this hall is too crowded for me. I gave your friends the address, and they've already left. Do you want to ride with me, Anna?"

"If you don't mind, Mr. Roberts, I'd like to go with Karl. Sentimental moment and all that."

"No, I don't mind; I understand. Anna has my address, Karl, so we'll see you there."

In spite of the drizzle, Anna walked to the car. She did not want to wait alone for Karl to bring the car around.

Moving through the crowd and stepping to avoid puddles kept the two occupied while they made their way to the curb. As he helped her into the car, he noticed the square box she carried.

"A gift from someone?" he asked, brushing the moisture from his jacket sleeves.

Anna offered the card from the top of the box, and there, in precise handwriting, Karl read, "Congratulations, Fraulein. As ever, John Smith."

The falling rain made snake-like paths down the windshield, and the red and green traffic lights reflected off the shiny hood. People hurried past the parked car by twos and threes, and snippets of their conversations filtered into the weighty silence.

Finally Anna spoke. "You are thinking just what I suspected before tonight, but I came to the conclusion whatever is in that box is not dangerous. At least it would not be an explosive, because he'd have no way of knowing when or where the box would be opened. I think if, or maybe I should say when, he shows his hand, I'm sure it will be done quietly. This time he'll want no witnesses."

Slowly she removed the wrapping, and there in red tissue lay a set of white mugs. Each bore the words, "Beautiful Mecklenburg Bay." But the picture in their minds was not beautiful. It was a vivid recollection of a farmhouse, brave adults, very frightened children, and gunshots—always the gunshots.

Karl's voice was low and angry. "The nerve—the cruel, colossal nerve of the monster! There's no doubt he knows who we are, and he's sent his message to intimidate us. These are a warning to us, leaving us to guess what his intentions might be. He'd like to be able to pull our strings, like puppets, but we can't allow that. We've got to outsmart him. Anna this is war—again!"

Anna watched Karl's jaw clench and relax, clench and relax. Minutes passed as he struggled for control. Without taking his eyes from the dripping windshield, he reached for Anna's hand and said, "The thing I vowed we would not do may be our answer for now. You say he is always in the city Monday through Wednesday. What if we were to disappear Saturday night, and not tell anyone where we are going or any of our plans? We could be so vague to those who know us that if he inquired he might figure we'd run away."

"I don't exactly follow what you're suggesting, but if you mean just pick up and leave, what do I do about Mr. Roberts? If I ask for some time off, I'll have to give him a date when I'll be back. I'll have to tell him something," Anna rationalized.

Karl rubbed the back of his neck to soothe some of the tension. "You'll tell him the truth, or at least enough of it to give him a reason to keep your plans to himself. Tell him Smith has become a nuisance. Tell him you'd appreciate it if he didn't let Smith know any part of your going or coming. He'll jump to conclusions, but for now we'll let that be."

Now it was Anna's turn to sit, analyze, and reach a conclusion. "I'm sure Mr. Roberts would give me a few days away—but," and she halted, ""how can we find a place to hide?" The word made her draw in her breath, but she continued, "I have tomorrow. I could check into places and transportation."

"We must do it. I can't see any other way for now. And no, we had better get to Mr. Robert's place, or he will wonder again if I've disappeared and taken you with me. What is his address?"

Anna's employer met them at the door and invited them into his home, bright with decorations. In that moment there was the strange thrust from morbid to merry. The worry and plans of the last half hour had to be pushed aside to make room for the comfort and security of those who meant them no harm. Shouts of "Congratulations!" and "Well done!" filled the room, and Anna responded with a grateful smile. Questions about her future plans, made out of kind interest, reminded her that even in this haven there lurked in the shadows the grim, dark form of Mr. Smith.

Mr. Roberts, unaware of the struggle, said, "Too bad Mr. Smith couldn't stay, for he certainly has taken an interest in our Fraulein. I suppose that is only natural, since they are from the same part of Germany."

"Oh? And where is that?" someone asked.

"Why, I believe he said it was the northeast, the district of Pomerania. Is that right, Anna?"

"That's strange, Mr. Roberts. I don't think he ever asked me, and I'm afraid I'll have to confess I haven't been nearly as interested in his background as he has in mine," Anna said with control.

"That's not a surprise, my dear. Smith has a remarkable ability to observe and listen, and that's what makes him so good at what he does."

A shiver swept over Anna. At this moment there was the temptation to blurt out their story and unmask this Jekyll-and-Hyde Smith. It was the fear that others would be drawn into his net that forced her to be silent.

As Roberts responded to someone's question, Kirstin drew Anna aside. With her usual enthusiasm, she said, "Jon and I would like to invite you to come to our home in the mountains. Karl tells me you have tomorrow off, so we thought you would appreciate a day away from the city. Wouldn't you like to come up and spend the night, so you could wake up in that fresh mountain air?"

Anna hesitated. Remembering the conversation in the car and wondering why Karl had not squelched the offer, said, "I don't know. I have some pressing business to take care of. The offer is more than enticing but ..."

Kirstin interrupted. "Karl told me you'd be torn between duty and pleasure, but he said I should encourage you to come. He'll bring you back in the afternoon. Wouldn't you like to come?"

Anna looked around, hoping for a nod of approval from Karl, but his back was to her.

Deciding, she replied, " I'll come. I'd be happy to come, and thank you for the invitation."

The rain had changed to wet dripping fog when the guests began to leave, and as Karl and Anna pulled away, he asked, "Do you want to go to your dorm for some clothes?"

"No, I'll take Kirstin's suggestion that I use some of hers; they'll fit, and it will save driving across town. I may be losing tomorrow morning's precious time to work on our plan, but I am so thankful for this time away from the city. Karl, when Mr. Roberts was telling everyone about Smith's knowledge of my past, didn't you wonder what else he may have told him? He apparently has laid the groundwork for evidence of a great friendship between us. We'd better be wary on this account too. I wonder why, except for the dinner date, he has avoided direct contact with you, Karl. Is he cowardly or clever?" Anna asked.

"For now, we'd better assume he's clever. You're right about the contact with me, but I was stupidly oblivious to the fact until you pointed it out. We are in this together, then and now. That man has no idea of the bond he forged between us that day," he reassured her.

Quietness and a measure of contentment filled the car. Karl's tone was warm when he said, "I don't remember ever telling you how much I appreciate you. It's long past due, but I want you to know that you are a very special person to me."

Modestly she said, "Thank you. I'm glad you said it, but from the first day, when there was no one but us, I've never questioned your love, or your ability to take care of me ... when I needed it," she added with a grin. "God has truly given us great blessing in our friendship."

He squeezed her hand, and as he returned his hand to the wheel, he breathed a prayer of gratitude. He knew that at the first awareness of Smith Anna had drawn herself away from God. It wasn't denial of His existence or His presence; it was a bitter outcry that the One who could have prevented it had allowed a man like Smith to exist and even now was permitting him to bring chaos into their lives. Her naturally independent spirit concluded she'd have to solve this problem herself, and turning her back on God, and his promises, she'd rebelled. Whenever Karl had tried to encourage her that God had not forsaken them or that He was able to protect them, there had been no assent. The response was always the same: no words, only eyes that blatantly stated, "I can't believe that." To hear Anna give God credit for their relationship was a tiny, promising fracturing of the barrier she'd built.

From his heart he prayed, "Heavenly Father, You are able to protect us from the man; Lord, please ease this heavy burden Anna carries. In Your mercy show her You are trustworthy." His thoughts went from prayer to phrases of Scripture, and the lines across his forehead began to soften. Anna watched the changing expression and knew from experience that Karl was working out things with the Lord.

The lights along the highway had gradually decreased as they neared the mouth of the canyon leading to the place in the mountains. Traffic was scattered, and as they drove into the patchy fog it seemed they were alone in a cloistered world.

"23 miles from this point to home," Karl informed her. "It's a winding road and sometimes narrow, but there aren't many cars, and this late on a miserable night we probably won't meet even one. Sometime, in the daylight, we will go to that miniature village you can faintly see through the trees."

She caught a glimpse of the midget buildings as the car lights swept the roadside.

"Wow!" They chuckled at her slang. It felt good to laugh together, and the spontaneity of it was an antidote for the solemn part of their evening.

"Didn't you tell me about a creek that runs parallel to this road?" Anna asked.

"Yes, and between the runoff and the rain, it will be up, but this road never does cross it, because farther on we go to the right, and the creek goes to the left."

"What is *runoff*?" she asked.

"Run off? That's the ordinary term that could mean leaving someplace in a hurry—" he stopped, realizing this attempt at humor was a barb. Starting again, he said, "Runoff, my dear lady, is the water that runs off the hills and mountains when the snow melts. In the spring the warm weather turns those melting snowbanks into steams and small waterfalls, which go downhill until they gather and join a creek. Even this cold rain helps melt the snow."

"You are amazing, Mr. Know-it-all, but I am proud of you for learning about these American mountains and sharing with me. This wonderful country is surely be coming home to us, is it not?" Her voice held a note of desperation.

Karl nodded his head, for he could feel Anna looking at him.

Headlights showed in the rearview mirror. Their approach blinked in and out of the mirror as Karl carefully negotiated the wet canyon curves. Gradually the approaching car was gaining, and knowing there was a short straightaway ahead, Karl slowed to let the driver pass. The rear car slowed too.

"He must not know this road, or he'd be passing us. There isn't another good place for miles. We'll both take it easy in the canyon tonight."

The thickening fog forced Karl to slow even more, and as he turned the defroster on, he wished the car behind wouldn't follow so close.

"Karl, that car is almost on our bumper!" Anna cried.

Chapter

18

"I DON'T KNOW WHAT THE man is thinking! We are going as fast as we dare, but it wouldn't do any good to slow down now, because we can't pass anyway," Karl said.

It was slight, but Karl felt when the other car brushed the bumper. *What is this driver, an idiot?* There it was again, and this time Anna felt it, for she grasped the armrest and stared at Karl. There was no mistaking it; the car was intentionally ramming them. As Karl gently pushed on the accelerator, the car responded, and for just a breath the pursuer fell back.

"That driver has to be out of his mind to try tricks like that. It would be foolish anytime, but on this road, tonight, it could be deadly!"

Anna asked, "How far is it yet to Jon's?"

Karl opened his mouth to speak, but no words came. The car was coming behind them with reckless speed.

"Pray, Anna!" he shouted, and put pressure on the gas pedal.

The car moved ahead, but this time the follower surged forward to fill the gap.

"I hope I have an advantage, knowing the road. Hang on!"

Their headlights pressed into the fog, and Anna hoped Karl would remember every curve. For a second the tracker's headlights would disappear, but each time the two beams would return, stabbing through mist. Gifts clattered to the floor from the backseat, but Anna made no effort to rescue them. With one hand on the dash and the other clinging to the armrest, she braced herself as they swung around the bend.

Karl turned too wide on the curve, and without hesitating the stalker pulled between him and the mountain. Just a few feet and he'd force them over the edge and down into the canyon below.

A brief flash of headlights against the rocks signaled a car coming down the slope, and immediately the rear driver slowed enough to let Karl swing back into his lane. As he glanced in the mirror to make sure the car was out of his way, the intent of the pursuer registered. This was not a drunk driver or a stupid jokester; this was a premeditated chase. Whoever was in that car had meant to force them over the cliff, but the oncoming car had prevented him. Why had he stopped short of his purpose? He could have pushed them off the road and over the embankment to their death, but he had stopped.

The oncoming car! The driver coming down the hill would have seen it all. Whoever was in that car would have been a witness!

"God!" Karl called out. If there had been time for more prayer, Karl would have identified the man and cried for protection, but the one name spoken was all there was time for. It was as clear as if someone had explained it to him. He and Anna were together on a nearly deserted, rain-slick mountain road, on a night with near-zero visibility. It was the perfect setup for a fatal accident.

Desperately Karl reasoned that he'd driven this highway day and night and knew every turn and grade. To be sure, visibility was poor, but he would have to take a chance on the plan that was forming in his head. It couldn't be more than a mile to the sharp curve and the top of the long hill. If he could gain even a few yards, they would momentarily be hidden by the mountain and could cut across the highway and onto the county road. He'd have to pull ahead, pray there were no approaching cars, and at the precise instant switch of the lights, swing left, and fly up the graveled side road. Once off the highway, they'd find a driveway that could conceal them.

He held his speed until he figured there was about a quarter of a mile until the curve. "Hold tight!" he shouted.

The car jumped ahead, and a second later he took one hand off the wheel to switch off the headlights. He'd seen the turnoff and, without slowing, shot across the highway and up the road. The car rocked as it slid in the gravel. Slowly Karl eased off the gas as they moved up in the darkness of the forest.

Chapter

19

IN THE DAYLIGHT HOUSES WERE visible from the highway, but in the fog and darkness even the driveway reflectors failed to glow. Slowing, Karl and Anna passed what appeared to be a mailbox. Karl braked and backed. An audible sigh escaped as he pulled into a lane and steered the car under the wet trees. Switching off the engine, he leaned back against the seat and shut his eyes.

"Mr. Smith," Anna whispered.

Except for the dripping moisture, there were no sounds, and even though there were houses nearby, the persistent rain and fog blotted out any lights or activity. They should have felt secure in the dark closeness of the car, but rather they felt trapped. Several minutes passed, long enough for the damp solitude to penetrate the car occupants' troubled thoughts and heighten their sense of fear.

Anna realized she was still gripping the armrest. With effort she brought her hands together and clasped them in her lap. The movement, however deliberate and slow, helped her relax. She let her tense shoulders drop and took a deep breath.

Opening her mouth to let the air escape she was about to repeat the action when she shattered the silence with a shriek. This time her hands flew to the dash, and with eyes tightly closed she screamed and screamed. Karl jerked around and threw up his arm as if to ward off a blow. In the second it took to move across the seat, he realized what Anna had seen. His arm fell and lay across her hands. "Anna! Stop! It's okay. Stop, Anna! Open your eyes and look."

Reluctantly she opened her eyes but kept her hands pressed against the dash. On the hood stood a large, wet cat with its triangular nose pressed against the windshield. The dim light from the gauges inside the car reflected off its eyes, turning them to yellow marbles. A sound like a hiccup escaped from Anna's throat when the animal raised its wide paw to swipe at the falling rain on the glass. Finally, curiosity satisfied, the cat padded to the edge of the hood and, dropping to the ground, disappeared in the dark.

"Only a cat!" The words came out in a rush of air as she pulled her hands back from the dash.

The car was growing cold in the wet night air, and Anna fumbled to button her sweater. Even though her fingers shook, the moving about began to break away the grip of fear. She retrieved her fallen purse and began to straighten the contents.

Karl spoke. "I'm sorry. I saw the cat jump up on the car, but I was so occupied with my thoughts I didn't realize you hadn't seen him too."

Silence again.

When Karl spoke, his voice was as chilling as the night air. "I think, after what we've gone through tonight, we can be sure of two things. We are not safe when we are together, and Smith wants seclusion when he tries to do away with us." He paused and then continued, "It's best if we don't go to Jon's. The risk is too great for us, and we could involve them. I've got to get you back to the dorm, where you'll be safe, and I'll get a hotel room."

Anna nodded her head.

"If we follow this dirt road around to where it connects with the highway, we can make a run for the city. Think you can handle another ride, Anna?"

"I can handle it." *Only in the sense of having survived once again.*

Karl backed out the driveway, and waited until he was straight in the road before he turned on the beams. Although there was the risk of meeting up with Smith, they eventually left the gravel and followed the main highway down the canyon. There were few cars, and as they pulled up to the dormitory, Karl asked, "When you get to your room, will you call Jon and Kirstin? Tell them we changed our mind about coming up. Just say we've decided to stay in the city and that I'll call them tomorrow. I'll call you in the morning. Be careful, Schatz."

"Don't walk with me to the door, Karl. Let me go by myself."

He watched her turn the key in the lock and disappear up the stairs. Fifteen minutes later he closed the door of a hotel room and stood looking at the telephone. There had to be someone who could help them. Not friends. If he or Anna confided in anyone, it would spread the danger. "God, Heavenly Father, what should we do? If we run, it will only prolong what seems the inevitable, but how can we deal with this danger? Show us, Father, what to do."

Thoughts and ideas rolled around in his mind. He picked up the hotel Bible that lay in the nightstand drawer and turned to the prophet of Isaiah. Flipping through the pages, his eyes fell on a part of a verse underlined by someone before him. He read, "When the enemy shall come in like a flood, the Spirit of the Lord shall lift up a standard against him." A flood—that's what this situation felt like, and it seemed the enemy was about to drown him and Anna. Looking at the pages of the book, he prayed, "Father, You know that, don't You? You will take a stand against him. I wish I knew how You are going to oppose Smith, but Heavenly Father, I believe You will. I will believe Your promise."

He lay down and began sorting through the events of the night. Had it been only six hours since he'd picked up Anna at her dorm for graduation? It seemed much longer. Tomorrow they'd make their plans for a few days absence, and unless the Lord showed them an alternative, they would do everything they could to make it look like they'd vanished. It was probable that Smith wouldn't fall for their ruse, but it was worth a try.

"Somehow, Father, You'll make it all work out," he prayed, and he began to sing in his off-key voice, "Great is thy faithfulness,

Oh God, my Father ..." and before he finished the verse, his voice trailed off and he was asleep.

Karl didn't know a disguised gentleman with an English accent had passed the hotel minutes after he had parked his car, and the man's keen eye had caught a glimpse of the white car he'd followed up to the canyon. While Karl lay in the quiet of his room, John Smith stood in the lobby and signed his name in the hotel register.

Chapter

20

A LIGHT CAME ON IN a room overlooking the parking lot. A tall figure stood at the window.

"How very fortunate!" Smith congratulated himself as he looked down at Karl's car. "And how cooperative the desk clerk to check if both my friends checked in or if only Mr. Karl Mann arrived. I suppose Anna is at her dormitory—they would feel safe with that arrangement."

The man regarded this unexpected stroke of luck as compensation for the aborted plan of a few hours ago. Since he was an obsessively patient man, he would carefully regroup, reconsider the possibilities, and try again.

Tomorrow he would follow Karl, and perhaps, if he and Anna met, there would be another opportunity. He would wait. But a frown crossed his broad forehead; he had taken these days away from his Chicago commitments, and this would be wholly unsatisfactory if the time was wasted.

With his eye he measured the distance between his Mercedes and Karl's car and noted there were no visible obstructions between the two. In the morning, he could sit unobserved in his car and wait. Yes, regrettably, it was probable the two had figured out it was he who nearly ran them off the road, and suspecting that, they would know he was still in town. They would, however, not know he was so near.

Even in the privacy of his room, he stood straight and tall, with hands clasped behind his back. It was unthinkable to slouch! It had never bothered him if others chose to droop; that was normal, but he was not like other men. He allowed only the conduct he envisioned as flawless behavior. He drew the drape and carefully hung his suit and shirt. Now for a few hours' sleep.

Chapter

21

A VOICE OUTSIDE THE DOOR called, "Housekeeping!"

From a deep sleep, Karl called, "No!" He could hear the maid's retreating steps, and the fading noise was a comfort to him. He was safe, and he felt sure Anna was too.

Nine thirty! A quick call to the *Timberline* took care of any questions about the day, and no one answered at Kirstin's. He dialed Anna's number and recognized the voice that responded, "Hello."

"Kirstin?"

"Hi, Karl. Surprised? Anna needed help packing to move to her apartment, so I showed up. We're about finished and are starving. Care to see that we're fed?" Her cheerful voice and conversation about ordinary needs pushed aside the serious problems of the day.

"Be happy to," he replied. "Give me half an hour, will you?"

She answered, "Fine. We'll be at the dorm."

A shower helped clear Karl's mind. There were plans to make, and until God led in another direction, they would continue with last night's decision. He didn't want to run, and to hide was repulsive, but for now they would do it. We would not make it easy for Smith.

He pulled open the drapes and filled the room with sunshine. Blue skies had replaced last night's rain clouds, and as he watched the city move below him, he enjoyed a measure of peace. Yes, God had protected him and Anna last night, and this day they would trust Him to show them where to go and what to do. There was hope.

After work on Saturday, they'd leave the city and go as far away as four days would allow. They'd choose the destination today, but the immediate business was to take the two girls to breakfast and, after eating, find a way to send Kirstin on her way. They would not let her get involved in their retreat.

In the few minutes before he left the room, he dialed Lisal's number.

"Hello."

"Good morning, Lisal. How are you today?" Karl asked.

"Good morning, Karl. I'm doing well, so well that I'm walking without a wrap on my ankle. No need for wheelchairs or crutches, but there are some colorful bruises. How was Anna's graduation last night? I have a gift for her that I'd like you to pick up when you come to town. I think this will help her know Lisal is a real person, not a figment of her friend's imagination."

Karl answered, "I'm in the city now, and I'd be happy to be the delivery boy. We're helping Anna move into her apartment today, but I'd like to work it out so you and I could have dinner. Can you manage a trip to eat out?"

"I would love to go with you, but this would not be … a good evening. Could you drop by so I could give you Anna's gift?" she asked.

Karl did not try to disguise the disappointment in his voice, and he persisted, "I'll be in again on Saturday. Maybe lunch?"

"Yes, maybe," Lisal hedged.

Karl said, "I'll be by later today. Shall I bring Anna with me?"

"One of these days we'll meet," Lisal said, "but not today. I'll be looking for you."

After the goodbyes, Karl realized how much he wanted to see her. It wasn't only concern for her injuries that drew his attention; no, it was far more than sympathy. He cared for her—more than cared—and with that realization came a rush of pleasure. He had strong feelings for Anna, Jon, and Kirstin, but was brought up short by the question of whether Lisal cared for him. He didn't know the answer, but for now, to admit he loved her was enough.

The half hour Kirstin had agreed on was past. Karl raced through the room, making sure he'd left nothing. A quick stop at the desk finished his stay.

The unexpected heat convinced him to shed his jacket and toss it to the backseat. There on the seat and on the floor were the scattered results of last night's wild ride. The danger had been real, but in the daylight, with the street noisy with passersby, he could push away the fear. In its place a smoldering anger lay. It was not a lashing-out feeling but the dull, heavy ache of the question, "Why?" Why was Smith in their lives again? Why was John Smith permitted to duplicate their previous defenseless position? They were no more able to protect themselves from him now than they had been when they stood facing him at the orphanage. Why, God? There was no flash of revelation, only a quickening of the conviction that he and Anna must carry out this day's plan.

As he pulled out of the parking lot, a gray Mercedes moved into the traffic a car's length behind him. If he'd checked the mirror he would have seen the car follow him the four blocks to the campus. But unaware, Karl squeezed into a parking place in front of the emptying dorm. It would take a minute longer, but to save Anna from the reminder and to keep Kirstin from asking questions, he'd have to pick up and put the packages in the trunk. Carelessly he gathered an armload and hid them away. Only a book and the picture mugs were left, and as he leaned across the seat to reach them, a voice called out, "You're almost on time!"

Backing out of the car and straightening, Karl stood clutching the gifts. Anna silently looked at the square box while Kirstin rattled on about food. Oblivious to the attitude of Karl and Anna, she stopped mid-sentence and teased, "Karl, why are you wearing those wild suspenders?"

Trying to match her mood, he quipped, "It's hard on one's credibility if pants fall down!"

Grateful for the moment to regain composure, Anna joined the banter, and with an artificial laugh took the mugs from Karl's hands.

"Kirstin, let me give you a thank-you gift, guaranteed new, just opened last night, in appreciation for your help this morning."

Raising her hands to refuse the gift, Kirstin said, "You don't owe me any thanks; it's been my pleasure to help you. Anyway, I couldn't take your graduation gift."

Anna held out the box to her. "I'd be more than pleased if you'd take these. Look, the scenes are of Germany, and they are quite beautiful. I know you enjoy coffee at your house, and you would make me very happy if you would take these mugs."

Reluctantly, Kirstin took the box and said, "If you change your mind, you know where they are."

"I'm positive I'll never want them," Anna said with conviction.

After they'd eaten, Kristin left them, just as Karl had hoped she would.

Anna asked, "Where can we go to make our calls? We'll need some privacy and a phone book."

"My bank has a courtesy phone in the lobby. I've never seen anyone use it, so if we monopolize it for several minutes, no one would be bothered. Even if it's in the middle of the activity of banking, we'll have privacy. Who'd notice us?" he asked.

He was almost right. No one inside the bank was interested in their presence. People passed by the lounge area, but Karl and Anna made their getaway plans undisturbed. They would fly out Saturday night and return next Thursday morning; they would tell no one of their departure, destination, or return. No one must be aware of the details or the plan, neither Mr. Roberts, or Jon, or Kirstin. Karl didn't mention Lisal.

Satisfied they'd accomplished all that was possible, they returned to Anna's apartment, and while she emptied boxes, Karl replaced the door lock and added a security chain. From the second-story window he examined the parking lot for safety hazards, and satisfied with the number of light poles close to the building, he was convinced the street and parking was as safe as they could hope.

"Anna, I am going to run out for a couple of hours. Anything you need?" he asked.

"Can't think of a thing. What I do need is a little time to get order out of this chaos," she told him with a grin.

"I'll see you about dinnertime then. We'll eat sandwiches somewhere. *Auf Weidersehen.*" And he was gone.

As the door closed, she heard the click of the new lock. She must remember to thank Karl. Drawn by an irresistible desire, she crossed the room and fitted the shiny key in the lock. She opened the door and looked down the hall. It was empty. Twisting the key, she watched the dead bolt slide out of its casing and, reassured by the sturdy length of it, returned it and closed the door. She slipped the key into her pocket and turned back to the room. Anna caught her breath, for it seemed, just for an instant, that she was a little girl again, standing in an upper room, alone. The scene was familiar, and yet this room was unlike the attic room in the house in West Germany. Reflecting, she dropped to the floor and leaned against a trunk. Drawing knees to chest, she wrapped her arms about her legs and, going along with the flashback, began to recall long-forgotten details, details that had led her back to that first upper room.

Incredible, she thought, *that we survived that year after the orphanage. It is more than incredible—it is a miracle! How many times God protected us from danger!* She paused and frowned. *Those days are over. Past. How can God allow now—*she stopped. *I'm not going to ruin this day by worrying about tomorrow.*

The one thought hardened the expression on her face to a set jaw and clenched teeth, and the hold on her bent legs tightened to an uncomfortable stiffness. "I should get up and bury these thoughts in work," but she continued to sit, and gradually, memories began to displace the present.

She saw a boy just reaching his teens and a smaller girl, begging for food and searching out barns or deserted houses to serve as shelter.

How did Karl ever discover we might be able to cross the line into the Western side? She answered her own question. *It must have been by listening to every conversation around us. He was good at that. While my mind was filled with fears, he must have been collecting bits of information, so he could figure a way of escape. How naïve I was, and how much I took for granted, while he bore the burden of taking us from East to West Germany. It truly was a miracle when he found a home for us with the Oldenburgs. The exchange was simple; we got a room, food, and schooling, and they got strong, young backs for work on their farm.*

To this day, Anna was unaware that to an observer her memories of the good years would seem dismal and bleak. It had been their way of life: hardly enough food to satisfy hunger, labor almost beyond a boy and girl's capacity, and the capricious gremlin of fear that always lurked in the back of their hearts.

All these circumstances had been acceptable because she and Karl had been given the attic room with a window and a stout door. That gray box, bare except for two cots, had been their fortress of security. Anna smiled to herself. *How carefully Karl used to close that strong lockless door whenever he'd leave me alone.*

But then, she tittered, *I shall never forget the day he made the wall! How did he do that?* She cocked her head to one side and searched her memory for the details; then she laughed out loud. He had used nails, a rope, and some cloth. She'd tried never to complain about anything, but one day, as if he knew it was necessary, he'd made the partition. It came back to her and as if it were yesterday she remembered. It had been just before an evening meal that he'd come upstairs and laid on his cot a hammer, two long nails, and a bundle of worn cloth. Because he'd worked without an explanation, she'd sat silently and watched as he dragged his cot to the room's center. Without asking her to hand him the supplies, had climbed up and down until, after many adjustments had made his solution for separate rooms.

"For you, Fraulein Anna," he had said with grave sincerity.

An uncertain, solemn thank you was her only expression. But that night, in the darkness, she'd wondered why she had thanked him for shutting her away from him.

Until they were ready to go to the university, they shared the attic room with the worn curtain wall, and it was sometime between the making of it and leaving it that she realized and appreciated the gift Karl had provided. It still was a puzzle, however, how Karl talked Mrs. Oldenburg into giving him that material!

"No wonder," she thought, "that I give Karl all the affection and loyalty I'd have given parents and siblings. I simply return the love he's given me."

"We love Him because He first loved us." The line of scripture tenderly and softly invaded her thoughts, and Anna sat motionless. For the past months she had chosen a mindset that refused to accept God's goodness and love. The recent fearful events were cruel and dangerous, and because she was blaming God for permitting them, she knew she not only allowed but encouraged rebellion against Him. She couldn't confide her bitterness even to Karl, because alongside the willful resentment was the depressing burden of guilt for allowing this attitude.

The love relationship she had enjoyed she had abandoned; in its place was a misery like she had ever suffered.

Tears stood in Anna's eyes, and she would have turned her attention back to the room, but the examination of her spiritual warfare would not be pushed aside. It seemed one part of her screamed, "Why?" and another, quieter voice pleaded for restoration to the sweet fellowship with her Heavenly Father.

The war in Germany had stolen from her a papa's loving touch and tender words. It was only after trusting Him as her Savior that she began to perceive God as a very real and empathetic

Heavenly Father. As understanding of him developed, she often made a picture in her mind of climbing onto her Father's lap and delighting in the security and favor of His presence. As a young girl, it had never come to her that some might think this imagining to be sacrilege, but as she matured, she realized it was He who had instigated that comforting association that had met her need.

"He first loved us …"

The words formed again, and with them the Holy Spirit's reminder that God loved her still and that He had never failed her. Not once!

Anna felt the urge to argue with the gentle voice, but instead she reluctantly admitted the foolishness of denying the truth of God's faithfulness. Incidents of His provision and care swept through her mind. He had protected her at the orphanage, taken care of her as she and Karl had crossed miles of danger in East Germany to safety, given them provision in a farmer's home until they were old enough to go out on their own, brought them to America, and over and over provided money to take them where they needed to go.

Minutes passed as she recalled the last 12 years of her life, and then finally she said aloud, "God, it's as if I have to make up my mind to trust You, isn't it? I have to decide to trust You for this part of my life too."

The room was quiet, and the young woman sat motionless in the warmth of the afternoon sun. Then, with a sob, she laid her head on her folded arms and cried, "Father, forgive me. Forgive my rebellion and stubbornness. Dear Heavenly Father, I cannot live without the joy of Your presence. This fear of Mr. Smith … I trust You to take me—us—safely through this hard time. Please protect us from him, and Lord, if it pleases You, would You remove him from our lives? We need Your help! *Oh, Gott!* You know I love you!"

The slanting rays of the late-day sun fell across the figure on the floor, and peace filled the room.

Chapter

22

IMMEDIATELY AFTER HE CLOSED ANNA'S apartment door, Karl's thoughts turned to Lisal. The sweet realization of his love for her filled his heart and mind, but even as he started the car and drove toward the Brown Palace, he began to be plagued by concern that she could reject him.

"What if she can see how I feel before I have the chance to explain to her? What if she has a boyfriend back home? What if she doesn't care a fig for me?"

It took two trips around the city block to find a parking place. That solved, he turned his attention to his wrinkled shirt smudged from carrying packing boxes. No cure for that, but he would use his comb. In spite of the unanswered questions, he walked with a light step to greet the doorman.

Down the block sat an idling, double-parked gray Mercedes. Its occupant watched Karl walk through the double doors of the hotel and wondered what would take a man like Karl, dressed as he was, into such a plush place. He was a patient man; he'd wait and see.

Lisal answered his knock with a smile and a "Come in." Maybe it was presumption, but she seemed so happy to see him he nearly blurted out the words that were foremost in his mind.

"You're looking great," he said instead.

"Thanks. I'm feeling good except for a few very sore bruises." She raised her arms to show the deep colors that spread from wrists to shoulders. "I think I must have hit every step with my arms."

She led him through the blue-and-white-tiled entry to the spacious sitting room and said, "Please. Sit down."

Karl lowered himself to the cream-colored sofa without speaking. He crossed his legs and continued his mental search for a neutral topic for conversation, but every choice ran right into the subject that was uppermost in his thoughts. He watched Lisal slowly bend and back into a chair, an involuntary grimace crossing her face. When she'd settled, she broke the silence with, "Did you get Anna moved into her apartment? What is it like?"

Thankful for the safe query, he grinned and answered, "Yes, we got her moved in. The apartment? It has four walls, not counting the partitions, ceilings, floors, several windows, and one door."

"Thank you, Mr. Lowell Thomas, for your vivid description. I can imagine just what it's like," Lisal said with a laugh.

He continued, "I'll take you to see it firsthand—don't they say a view is worth 10,000 words?"

"I think," Lisal corrected, "it's one *picture*, and yes, I'd like to see it." She added, "Does she have a roommate?"

He explained to her that rather than looking for someone to share a place had decided to take a small apartment and live alone. "The place is in a quiet area, and until she buys a car she can ride the streetcar to work. She is hoping Mr. Roberts can find a good deal on a car for her."

Lisal changed the subject by saying, "Speaking of car dealers, do you see anything of that Mr. Smith?"

Karl hesitated, trying to remember how much he'd told her about the man. "Yes, as a matter of fact, he came to Anna's graduation … but not to the party Mr. Roberts gave for her. Seems he leaves town on Wednesday nights … he probably had a flight to catch." He stumbled through the words, knowing it was only half true.

Lisal didn't seem to notice, but continued, "Is Anna still apprehensive about him?"

For Karl, almost any subject would be welcomed except Mr.

John Smith, so he answered with an affirmative and then asked, "How about your father? Is his business going well?"

Lisal seemed reluctant to change the subject. For an uncomfortable length of time she looked at Karl, but her bland expression revealed none of her thoughts. Shifting his weight to break the hush in the room, he watched her eyes, but at the same time noticed the slight shiver that moved her shoulders.

She blinked and spoke. "He is doing well. Too well. If all goes as he expects, we will be returning home next week."

Lisal leaving? All the words of the last minutes faded as Karl studied her face to see if there was a hint of sadness. He couldn't tell, but with swift determination, he knew he'd never let her leave without knowing of his love.

"When you say next week, do you mean Monday, or Friday, or when?" he asked knowing there was an edge of desperation in his voice.

She crossed the room and sat next to him. Smiling, she put her hand over his and said, "It won't be until the end of the week, I'm sure of that." She stopped and then, as if carefully choosing each word, said, "We have some matters to settle before we leave, so it seems Father will need to stay in the city for several days yet." Again she hesitated, and then realizing the effect of her words, she continued, "I want you to meet my father before we leave. Could you come to dinner, and would you like to bring Anna? Maybe Tuesday evening?"

A long intake of breath gave Karl time to put together the right answer. He knew it might be evasive, but by no means was he going to tell her he was temporarily leaving town.

He'd handle one problem at a time. First, the dinner with Lisal's father. He said, "Tuesday's not a good night for me. Could we make it next Thursday?"

"Thursday? I think that would be just as good," Lisal answered.

Karl's preoccupation blinded him to the girl's frown, and her suggestion, when she said, "I'll talk it over with Father, but I'm thinking this might be a good time to meet Anna."

Karl ignored the repetition of the invitation for Anna and went on, "Lisal, I don't want to think about your leaving. I knew you weren't here permanently, but you are leaving too soon." He stopped, and then said, "We'd better take advantage of every minute. Are you free tomorrow night?"

Slowly, as if considering the possibility, she answered, "Yes," and then "I can be."

"Good. I'll pick you up at seven."

He took her hand as they walked to the door. If only he could take her in his arms, but instead he lifted her hand to his lips and kissed her fingertips.

"'Til we meet again, Fraulein." And he was gone.

Chapter

23

It HAD BEEN ONLY 24 hours since Karl had sat in the office working at the typewriter, but it seemed much longer. The familiar surroundings made the previous night and day seem unreal. Making request for a few days off brought the danger into sharp focus.

He jumped when the editor spoke to him; Mr. Bigelow raised his shaggy eyebrows but said nothing. But a little later he said gruffly, "I hear by way of the grapevine there's a big West Coast paper looking for a staff writer. I'm loony to tell you this, but this may be your chance. Want the address?"

Karl mentally pushed through the jumble of Mr. Smith, Lisal, and ideas for this week's column before he comprehended the offer.

"Why, yes, sir. I would appreciate that address."

This would be the appropriate time to express how much he appreciated the work at the *Timberline* and how grateful he was for the editor's wise council. But he also knew Bigelow would have waved aside the remarks. This abrupt bit of information was the old man's way of wanting Karl to understand that he liked his work, that because he had confidence in him he'd suggested the step up. He would never say those words. So, Karl smiled and said, "Thanks, Mr. Bigelow. I'll send a resume."

The older man's face softened, but with the same gruff voice said, "Thought you'd like to know," and laid the address and precisely typed and signed reference on the typewriter.

A low whistle escaped from Karl's lips as he read the name of the Los Angeles paper. *This is major league stuff,* he said to himself and grinned. His mind raced with thoughts and questions about the possibility of realizing his dream. He knew he would devote his life to writing, because he felt he had something to say. Journalism was not merely an occupation, it was his calling.

Leaning back in his chair, he pushed the hair off his forehead and let his thoughts wander, until in his mind's eye he could see his name under the bold black print of an editorial title. A parade of subjects marched by, and after an inspection of the topics, he concluded writing for the big-city crowd wouldn't cover any different concerns than what the small town folk worried about.

The girl from the front counter carefully put down a sheet of paper on Karl's desk and, with a wink, walked away. The handwriting was unmistakable. Before he'd picked it up, he guessed the sender and the message. He felt his neck and ears grow red. In a scrawl across the page were the words, "The way to make a dream come true is to wake up!"

With clenched-jaw discipline, he kept his eyes off the editor's cubicle. The front legs of his chair thumped to the floor as he methodically folded the note into a tiny square and dropped it into the scarred green wastebasket.

"That guy is ..." but Karl didn't finish the accusation. The note had accomplished Bigelow's goal. The daydreaming and the worrying put aside, he focused on the keys in front of him.

It was five o'clock before he put the cover on his typewriter and cleared his desk. Time enough to get a shower and pick up Lisal at seven.

At home, he was surprised to see Jon walk into the kitchen. "Hey, Doc, what are you doing home at this early hour?" Karl asked him.

"Had a last patient cancel, so I hightailed it for home. I'd ordered some gravel for the driveway and thought it might come today. If

I don't do something about those ruts, we're going to have to park on the road! How about some coffee?"

"No thanks. I've got a date with the girl with the sprained ankle," Karl explained with a grin.

"I remember. When you have time, we'd like to hear about this lady. Is she special?" Jon asked.

Karl's grin grew, and asked Jon, "How special is Kirstin to you?"

"Extremely! Number one!" he replied.

Karl said, "To answer your question, she's that special!" Then, with an affected nonchalance, he added, "I'm taking a few days off starting tomorrow, and I'll be back for work next Thursday."

"Good for you," Jon said. "Business or pleasure?"

"You might call it a little of both." With that evasive answer and a wave, he left the house.

Minutes later Jon heard Karl's car start the slow descent to the road.

To Kirstin he said, "I've got to get that load of gravel and fill those ruts before we ruin our cars." How could he know that gravel would not just fill the ruts but fill Karl with the expectation of imminent disaster?

He continued, "What do you think is going on with him? It's obvious he's very interested in this girl, and he's happy about that, but there's something or somebody tightening the screws somewhere in his life. Can't be his job, because even old Bigelow's worried that he hasn't been his contented self for a couple of months. Has he given any idea what may be troubling him?"

Kirstin frowned, and her response was thoughtful. "Yes, I do know something that may be a problem. I'm not sure when it started, but a few weeks ago I heard a phone conversation between Karl and Anna. I wouldn't have paid any attention, except I caught a word or two that made me think Anna was in trouble. When he hung up I asked if she was having difficulties at work, and he told me she was upset because of a salesman. It's a weird story. Seems Anna suspects this man may have been one who committed a terrible crime, and as children they witnessed it. At the time of the call, Karl was afraid they might be in danger if what Anna supposed proved true. Only once more did the name come up, so I thought it had all blown over. Could be he's still trying to figure out if this is the man from their past."

"Karl's a level-headed man; if there was any real danger he'd get help. He knows how to handle himself. I'll catch him in the morning and ask him if there's anything we can do for him. Good thing he's taking a few days off. That's probably just what the doctor ordered," Jon said with a grin.

The evening traffic forced Karl to give full attention to the mountain road, so he felt, rather than saw, the escape route when he passed the dirt road. In the late afternoon sun there was no clue of the near disaster on that rainy night. But tonight, thoughts of Mr. Smith would not stifle his attention to Lisal. It was true the man was a very present threat on his and Anna's life, but whatever the future held for them, tonight Lisal must know of his love for her.

Chapter

24

LISAL WAS WAITING WHEN KARL rang the bell. He couldn't find the right words, so instead, he put his arms out and drew her to himself. There was no resistance, and after a quiet minute, she tilted her head and looked into his eyes.

"I love you, Lisal," Karl whispered.

"I love you, Karl," she replied.

He gently kissed her and found no resistance there either!

The evening passed too quickly for all the things they needed to say to each other. Must she leave with her father? Would he approve of Karl? What if Karl was hired by the newspaper on the West Coast—would that make a difference in their plans? It was late when they started back to the hotel.

Lisal said, "Karl, why don't you come by tomorrow noon, and we'll have lunch!"

Through the evening he had avoided any talk about the next few days, hoping he could find a plausible excuse for his absence. Now more than ever, he did not want Lisal aware of the danger from Smith.

"This is a rotten time for me to be tied up, but when I leave tonight I won't be able to see you until next Thursday. There isn't a way in the world I can meet you tomorrow. Please understand."

"I think I can," she said. "We'll plan on Thursday. Shall I tell Father about us?"

"Maybe a clue, but let's wait. I'd like to tell him when we are together."

"Will you call before Thursday?" she asked.

"I'll try," Karl promised, "but if I don't, remember that I'll be thinking of you always."

"What a strange thing to say, that you'll be 'thinking of me always'—you make it sound like we may never see each other again."

Karl pulled Lisal to himself and held her close while he searched for words of reassurance while keeping the truth from her.

"I don't want you to even consider that. I mean ... please understand that I may find it impossible to call, but that doesn't mean you won't be on my mind and my heart. I love you, Lisal."

"Karl, I'm sure everything is going to be all right," Lisal said softly.

What had he said to her that she was giving him assurance for the future? It was as if she had read his thoughts; he had to be careful with his words. Silence was the only safe response he could give.

"I love you, Karl," she whispered, "and I'll be waiting for you next Thursday."

"I don't want to leave now, and I don't want to be away from you until next week, but I must do both. Is your father in, Lisal?"

"He'll be back soon. I won't be alone all the time," she said.

"I must go, then. I'll miss you," Karl repeated.

She smiled and slipped her arm through his. "I'll miss you too. Do what you need to do and come back to me."

The elevator was empty, and in the lobby only a few late-nighters. In spite of the street light, Karl had a feeling of darkness, a sense that he should be watching over his shoulder. Only two parking spaces to his car. He was anxious to put the key in the lock and get in the security of his car. *So far the car has been the place I am least safe*, Karl thought. Just the same, a sigh of relief escaped as he swung out in the midnight traffic.

The gray Mercedes pulled into the hotel's underground parking.

No need to follow, for it was apparent Karl's destination was home. It would be easy enough to find him tomorrow.

The few cars on the city streets moved at a steady pace, because the lights were in their favor. The night was warm and clear, and as the brightness from the city fell behind, Karl could begin to pick out the twinkling stars against the night sky. He loosened his tie and the top button on his shirt and with the same hand reached over to switch on the radio. The words from the talk show caught his attention but held it for only a minute.

"It's not good," he said aloud, and he turned the knob until it clicked off. The car was as silent as the dark canyon he was entering, but he wasn't thinking of either the silence or the darkness. There had been something said in Lisal's room—something that now cast a shadow over the pleasure of the evening. What was it? What subject had the conversation touched that could possibly be more important than their first pledge of love? They had talked only of each other, of plans for the future, and had found joy in the knowledge that God had brought them both from Germany only to have their paths meet in this Western city. Why this feeling of apprehension? He would surely miss Lisal—there was no denying that. If there was any possible way to stay he wouldn't carry out the plan to leave, but this temporary separation, hard as it was, was not the demon that was plaguing him. There was something— no, some*one*—else that was the cause of this uneasiness that kept disrupting what should have been a happy frame of mind. Who, then, was it?

Karl thought through the evening's conversation and abruptly stopped. Lisal's father—the invisible man! Why had they never met? Was it because he was out of the city so often? Where did he go? Did it really seem Lisal was deliberately delaying their meeting, and if so, why?

Karl maneuvered a sharp curve, and when he could come back to his thoughts, he felt for one moment embarrassment that he should be questioning Mr. Schiller. The name, after all, was Schiller, not Smith. But both men, Schiller and Smith, were salesmen, both traveled between Germany and the United States, and for some reason, he had never been able to come face to face with either of them. Why was Mr. Schiller never in when he visited Lisal?

His grip on the steering wheel tightened and the line of his jaw hardened. "I must not think this way. There can be no connection. She is Lisal Schiller, not Lisal Smith. There are two German salesmen. The timing must be purely coincidental!" His fingers relaxed, and for a mile or two he drove letting his thoughts caress the memory of Lisal in his arms. Then, unbidden, her answer to his question about her father came back. What had she meant by, "He'll be back soon."? *Soon* as in this evening, or *soon* as in a few days—Sunday, maybe?

"Oh God! This can't be!" Karl moaned.

Chapter

25

AFTER HE LEFT THE CAR in the driveway and was lying in the quietness of his room, the only interruption to his distressing thoughts was the chimes of the clock as it counted off the early morning hours.

Near dawn he fell into a troubled sleep. When somewhere in his chaotic dreams an alarm sounded, he was immediately awake. It was only after catching a few words of Jon's conversation that Karl realized the ringing was the telephone. He lay back and let his head drop into the dent in the pillow, but when the screen door slammed he was sitting up with his feet on the floor. It was the familiar whine of Jon's car's engine and its gradual descent to the road that drove away the grip of fear in the last few minutes. He drew a deep breath and exhaled slowly.

A cool early morning breeze pushed through the curtains and brushed past Karl's bare shoulders. Rising, he drew the curtains and stood looking into the pink predawn light. Across the road, three elk grazed in a small meadow. Shadowed by the tall trees and unaware of his gaze, they leisurely fed, only occasionally raising their heads to check the wind for any scent of danger. As the light of the sun began to push the shadows back, the elk worked their way into the trees until they had disappeared. Minutes passed, and Karl turned from the panorama and slowly began choosing clothes to put in his suitcase. Karl used this time to gather hope that, just as the elk had eaten and then moved off into the shelter of the woods, he and Anna could just as easily slip off into some sanctuary.

Carefully he rolled clothes and filled his bag. With discipline, he was not allowing in thoughts of Lisal or her father. As hard as it was not to think of her, it was even more difficult to keep out questions of her father. Two men were blending into one. Was there a Schiller and a Smith?

His hand rubbed the stubble on his chin, and he headed for the bathroom. Resolutely, he said, "Today there is just a Smith!"

Packing, dressing, and straightening the room took more time than he'd planned, and hopes of leaving before Kirstin was up faded when he smelled the coffee.

He'd told her he'd be away a few days, and no doubt she'd remembered and decided to send him off with a "good breakfast!" He'd eat and somehow carry on a conversation that he knew would consist mostly of Kirstin's questions. No matter that her inquiries would be motivated by innocent interest; she must not know even one detail of the next day's strategy.

Kirstin was not in the kitchen as he passed through on his way to the car. He could just leave, but he knew he owed his friends more than that.

"Karl!" he heard her call. "Would you like a cup of coffee? It's ready."

Kirstin was surprised when he entered the kitchen from outdoors. "I thought you were in your bedroom," she said.

"No, I'm on my way. My suitcase is packed and in the car, and ready to go."

"We didn't expect you'd be leaving this early. Jon was hoping for some time with you this morning, but as I suppose you heard he was called away on an emergency."

"Tell him goodbye for me, will you? I'd better be going."

She watched his eyes as he talked and wondered if she should ask him if everything was settled with Anna. It was not his way to be abrupt or evasive.

"Karl, is everything good with you and with Anna? Has she solved the problem with the salesman? I'd taken for granted it was mistaken identity. Has it all worked out?" Kirstin asked with concern.

"There's nothing for you to be worried about. Don't even think about it. Someday I may tell you the whole story, but in the meantime just wish me happy travels."

He walked around the table and dropped a kiss on the top of her head. Smiling, he said, "Goodbye, Kirstin."

A frown creased her forehead as she replied, "Goodbye."

He was relieved to make a hurried exit.

A few miles toward the city he stopped at a phone booth. "Anna? You must be ready to leave for work, so I'll be quick. Are you packed? Good! Yes, I have my key to your place, so I'll pick up your bag. There are some plans we need to go over before this evening. Could you catch a cab this noon and meet me at that old overgrown park on 38th? Yes, I know it's a weird place, but we need to meet somewhere secluded."

There was a pause after he listened to her protests, but he interrupted with, "Sorry, Anna, but this is a precaution we must take. I'll be by the old concrete benches toward the north side. Okay? See you at noon."

He could hear the impatience in her voice as she agreed, but rather than continuing the conversation, he said goodbye and hung up.

Frustration and fear- deadly combination that would haunt them until this whole situation was settled. Best to forge ahead and settle disagreements later.

The bold words and colors on the travel agency's posters made Karl irritable. Today's circumstances stole the glamour and excitement from travel, and the word *Escape* across the picture of Rio brought a deep frown to Karl's face. By the time it was his turn at the counter, he resented the clerk's cheerful helpfulness; nor did he respond to her pleasant chatter. The trauma of retreat, the question mark that was Lisal's father, and his own struggling faith left him preoccupied. He resented any intrusion to his troubled thoughts. With no more than nods or grunts, he finished the transaction and stowed the tickets in his pocket. Because it seemed necessary, he hurried to the car, but once seated behind the wheel he couldn't decide whether to pick up clean shirts or get something to eat. A growl behind his belt buckle reminded him he'd had only coffee to start the day. The shirts could wait.

The possibility of a grinning waitress hovering over his table convinced Karl to find a fast-food drive-through. He parked under a nearby tree, where his mind laid out the pieces of his puzzle. They were all there except one, the one that would complete the picture. What would that final piece be?

Silently he prayed. "Father, I'm afraid and confused. It doesn't set right to be running away, even for a while, but You haven't shown us a different way, so is this what You want? How are You going to handle Smith and settle this threat to our lives?"

Word by word, a verse long ago committed to memory began to form: "Do not fear, for I am with you; do not look anxiously about you, for I am your God; I will strengthen you, I will help you ..."

Oblivious to the music from the drive-in and the cars around him, Karl bowed his head, and lifting his voice to God, he prayed, "Almighty God, this is Your word. You said You are with me in this, that You'll help me, and that You are going to take care of this problem with Your own hand. I can't guess how or when, but You never make mistakes, nor do circumstances ever get out of Your control, so here goes, Father. I commit Anna and myself to You and to Your care. In Jesus's name, amen."

The route to the meeting place in the park ran across the center of the city, and as Karl passed the library, he imagined Lisal coming down those great cement steps. "How could I doubt her? She said she loves me. If her father is my enemy, she must not realize it or even suspect. Yet ... What about the fall at the tower that kept me from being with Anna when she met Smith? Could that have been planned? Never! No one in their right mind would take a chance with a fall like that. It's all ... all what? Too many pieces of the puzzle that don't fit. And I've told her I love her. Could I truly love her if ..."

Enough!

The light changed to green, and Karl drove toward the deserted park.

Chapter

26

THE ENTRANCE TO THE PARK was blocked by orange and white barricades, so Karl drove around the block to a side street where he could leave his car. The neighborhood had the same uncared-for look as the park. The only sign of life was a sedan parked in front of one of the houses and a gray Mercedes that had passed him and turned at the next corner.

He slammed the door and started to walk away, but stopped and stood still. Turning, he drew the key from his pocket and, leaning down, locked the car door. He chided himself for apprehension, but at the same time admitted that the sight of any gray Mercedes rattled him. Once again he started across the overgrown park. The hot, unsympathetic noonday sun beat down on him.

The bushes and flower beds that once had been trimmed and weeded hadn't survived in the tangle of wild vines and briars. Karl stabbed his toe at the determined weeds that pushed their way up through the cracked asphalt pathway. Columned arches, once unique landmarks, now vandalized down to grotesque stubs, and looking at the ruin, Karl agreed with the city council—it would be best to put aside sentiment and plow up these acres. It was a neglected and cheerless place, haunted by the ghosts of ladies and gentlemen of the past.

Just a few hundred feet ahead were the once stately oaks sheltering the cement benches resting in twos with their tall backs leaning against each other. Well under the shadow of the trees, on one of the benches, Anna was waiting. She had taken him at his word when he'd suggested isolation. Ragged branches hung from the trees, and rows of abandoned shrubs made her nearly invisible. As soon as he saw her, he realized his eyes had been drawn there because she had been watching his approach. He raised his hand in a greeting but said nothing. It seemed necessary to maintain the silence of the place. They were face to face when he finally spoke.

He took her hand and said, "Sorry if it seems I'm dramatizing our problem, but we need to talk and make our final plans." Anna shivered, and he realized his bad choice of words. He didn't try to correct the selection; instead he raised his eyebrows and attempted a weak smile.

"Couldn't you have given me all the information on the phone?" she grudgingly asked.

Karl knew her irritation was her way to cover her fear, so he gently responded, "No, because I needed just to see you and give you your plane ticket. We'll be safer if we arrive at the airport separately, board separately, and not even sit together. We must stay as far apart as possible until we arrive in Canada. We'll assume Smith is out of town, but even so, let's be as cautious as we can. You need to ..."

"Karl!" Anna stiffened, and her fingernails dug into his hands. Looking past his shoulder her eyes widened as panic spread across her face.

"Karl," she gasped. "Look!"

Slowly Karl turned to face John Smith.

Chapter

27

THE FIRST EYE CONTACT WAS not what Karl would have imagined. He might have expected flaming, raging anger or maybe black, smothering terror, but instead he felt very much as he had when he'd first seen Smith. He was held by a grim foreboding and a maddening inertia.

The man casually walked across a small clearing, and as he came on, a little breeze tugged at the collar of his shirt. Frozen in place, Karl noticed the well-cut jacket was a conservative tweed and the trousers held a sharp crease. Smith wore polished penny loafers, each displaying a shiny new cent. The only sound was the snapping of scattered dead twigs as the brown shoes came closer.

Karl watched as the copper pennies approached and stopped a few feet off. Without seeing, he knew the face of Lincoln, the emancipator, was partially hidden under the slits in the smooth leather of the shoes. Then, as if awakened from a trance, his mind made a swift connection between that proclamation of freedom and his immediate need. He must not—he would not—be in bondage to this man! His memory and the present threat had enslaved him long enough. Karl raised his eyes and boldly looked into John Smith's face.

Before he could say a word, the quiet, accented voice said, "We meet again, Karl. Your name is Karl, is it not?" It was a statement more than a question, and without waiting for an answer, he went on. "How long has it been ?10,15 years? You have changed considerably from the boy at the orphanage." He paused, expecting some response.

Anna's face was pinched into a frightened mask, and Karl frowned and stared at the man's incredible control.

Smith continued, "You are surprised to see me." It was a declaration, and Karl drew from the inflection that he was telling them that their whereabouts had not been a mystery to him.

"Herr Smith, what do you want of us?" The brief words came out hard and brittle, and Smith, confident of his advantage, replied, "I don't think we need to be evasive or naïve about our ... shall we say, past experience? So I will be straight to the point."

He moved so the sun was at his back. "You know something about me that I cannot afford to have recalled."

As he changed a bulky roll of newspaper from his right to left hand, he shifted his weight and continued. "Because I cannot possibly trust you to forget that unfortunate incident, I am pressed to remove any possibility that you might betray me or reveal what you remember." An evil smile touched his handsome features. "Didn't I call you witnesses that day?"

He was enjoying the recollection, but slowly the smile faded, and he said, "At that time you were an asset to me; now you are a liability."

Anna broke her silence. "Mr. Smith, how did you know where to find us today?"

Looking at her, he dipped his head slightly as if finally acknowledging her presence. "My dear Fraulein, both of you are extremely easy to follow: your actions are innocently open and predictable. Last night, after watching Karl leave the city, I knew I could pick up the trail today by keeping track of you. You would be at Robert's showroom, and even if I parked my car nearby, it would have been quite unnoticed."

Without asking, Karl knew it was the same gray Mercedes that had passed him just minutes before.

Neither he nor Anna had taken their eyes from the man, so

when his look shifted from the two of them to the end of the bench, they followed his gaze.

A woman stood in the shadows. She wore untidy baggy slacks, a brown loose shirt, and a hat with a brim that flopped down to hide her face. She had come so silently she could have passed for a ghost from the past. Anna, who stood closest to the person, grasped Karl's arm in a response even Mr. Smith's appearance hadn't provoked.

From under the great gray hat, a feminine voice said, "Good afternoon, Herr Schmidt."

The speaker hesitated just long enough for her appearance and words to have their desired effect, and then she began again. "You will not remember me," she addressed Smith, and moving a little closer to Anna said, "but I will never forget you!" She stopped and waited for a response.

Involuntarily, all eyes turned to Smith.

The motionless, wordless silence held the four in a vacuum until the spell was broken by the salesman bending his right arm and resting his finger on the middle button of his tweed jacket.

When he spoke, the tone was ingratiating, "Indeed, Fraulein, and how is it you remember me, and may I ask from where?"

By now the woman had moved next to Anna, so she was partially hidden from Karl's view. Neither he nor Anna could see the face behind the hat, but when she spoke, they could imagine the fierce and grim expression. Her tone was low with restraint, but each word was perfectly clear.

"I know you from an orphanage in Germany."

The complacent posture stiffened as Smith's friendly façade disappeared.

The same question was in everyone's mind: *What could she mean?*

Karl and Anna were questioning, *"Our" orphanage? There are only two living people from that day and place, aren't there?*

Mr. John Smith spat out, "You are mistaken." Each syllable was like a savage blow aimed at the speaker, to intimidate and subdue.

Anna's fingers tightened around Karl's arm, and she felt the tensing of his muscles, but neither moved.

"No, Herr Schmidt, you are the one who is mistaken. Your plan to leave only two children to witness the execution of adults"—she paused to regain her control—"and the other children, did not succeed. You see, I was one of the dispensable orphans."

She stopped, deliberately waiting for the shock of her words to penetrate the iron man dressed in the soft tweed jacket.

"As an innocent little girl I faced your guns, but that day when you thought eleven were destroyed, one survived. You see, don't you, that you left three witnesses, not two."

The man stood frozen. The great consuming desire to control had suffered a blow. At no time in his life had he felt so threatened. When just a youth he'd carried off believable switch from communist to Nazi, and years later, when it was propitious, with the finesse of a master he'd regained his accreditation as the faithful communist. Now, when life had settled into a satisfactory routine, he was not going to tolerate this intrusion, nor would he accept any implication that somewhere his well-laid plans had misfired. That could not be. The unfamiliar feeling of intimidation was tightening its grip on his mind. How could he sort out his thoughts and dispose of this interference if he couldn't think! Without his usual deliberation, his right hand moved from the button on the jacket to the roll of newspaper. Even as he performed the action, he was not convinced it was his best choice, but from the dark recesses of his mind came the irresistible urge for survival. His hand closed over the metal of the gun, and slowly the tunnel of paper collapsed.

Chapter

28

KARL WHEELED TO PUSH THE women away as a shot split the silence. He fell against the two pushing them down onto the gray concrete bench, as he slid to the ground. Before his body settled into the tumble of weeds and grass, he raised his eyes to the slumped forms on the seat. Which one had been hit? He had not even been grazed by a bullet. Did he dare move? Did Smith still have the gun pointed at him—or them? Slowly he raised and looked at the figures sprawled on the bench. Neither seemed to have been hit; instead, both were staring beyond him.

Anna whispered, "Look at Smith!" The man in the tweed jacket and penny loafers lay face down in the barbs of the brittle underbrush.

Karl had been right about the seclusion of the area, for there were no shouts or running feet to check on the gunshot; there was only the dappled sunlight, the muted sounds of distant traffic and, from the tangle of trees, two approaching figures.

The girl next to Anna stood and—pulling off her hat—shouted, "Father!" and in a strangled voice said, "Thank you!"

Even as Karl watched the hat come off the woman's head and heard the familiar voice, it was several seconds before he could voice, "Lisal!" and the girl in the baggy pants turned.

"Yes! Oh yes, Karl! And this is my father." She stepped forward to meet the older man as she said, "I couldn't see you, Father, and I never did hear you come; for one awful second I thought Herr

Schmidt was going to win again." She stepped into his opened arms and let him, with crooning German, reassure her.

The second man, after replacing the gun in his shoulder holster, knelt to examine Smith.

"Is he dead?" Anna asked.

"Yes. Very."

"Karl," Lisal said, turning to face him, "this is my father, Marcus Schiller."

Two men—two separate men!

The older man moved forward and, stretching out his hand, said, "How do you do, Karl?"

"Mr. Schiller? How do you do?" The enormous question mark of the man's identity disintegrated, and with great sincerity he added, "I am very happy to meet you!"

A smile spread across Lisal's face as she said, "Anna, I am Lisal, and this is my father, Marcus Schiller, and our friend, Leo McDaniels."

The two women clasped hands and then, without hesitation, embraced.

McDaniels began to speak. "I'll call for an ambulance, and we'll get Schmidt out of here." He looked around at the circle of faces and said, "I think all of us will be relieved to see the last of this bird." He turned to make his way through the tangle of bushes.

Mr. Schiller said, "Let's sit down." He led the way around to the opposite side of the benches.

"Lisal," Karl started.

But Anna interrupted him with, "Lisal, you were one of the little girls at the orphanage?"

"Yes, I was. I was one of the children left for dead."

They could hear Leo returning, and sat in silence until he appeared. He said, "There's no need for you to stay around here. Go back to the hotel, and I'll meet you there after we get this cleaned up."

"We'll do that. We'll wait for you in our rooms," Mr. Schiller replied. To Karl he said, "Leo and I saw your car when we drove up. I'm parked a block or so north. Lisal and I will drive around and meet you and Anna there."

As Anna and Karl walked past the prone figure and toward the street, she was the first to speak. "How does Lisal fit into this? I know she said she was at the farm, but all these years, why would she have any ... why would she be involved with our ...? Karl, there are so many questions! I don't even know what to ask!"

Karl's only response was a quiet, "I know." If it was a nightmare before, it was as a dream world now. What questions? What answers?

Lisal was waiting at their car. "Why don't you leave your car here and ride with us? Father can bring you back later."

"Yes." Karl checked the doors to make sure they were locked. Looking up, he was relieved to see that Schiller did not drive a Mercedes.

For several minutes the group rode in silence, each reliving the last half hour. Finally Karl said, "I have so many questions, I don't know where to begin."

"Ask the most obvious one," Schiller prompted.

"Okay. How are you involved with Smith—or is it Schmidt?"

"*Involved* may be too simple a word, but I know what you mean. Do you want to start the story, Lisal, or do you want me to?" he asked his daughter.

"I'll start, Father. Anna, Karl, I know it will bring back painful memories, but we must begin years ago at the orphanage in East Germany. I, too, would have loved to forget, but for one thing. Herr Schmidt came to the farm he murdered the Christiansens, Mrs. Jensen, the Jewish man, and—he thought—seven children. I was one of those children who was shot, but my wound was not fatal. That night a member of the underground found me and took me to his home in the village, where he and his wife nursed me back to health.

A little over a year later, my father and I were reunited—that is another story—and we made our way to the West. That is a story much like what you experienced, I imagine. My mother had been killed in the war, so since our reunion my father and I have become inseparable. Except when I had to be in school, I traveled everywhere with him, and it was on one of those trips that I saw Schmidt. I was such a small child when he left me for dead that I couldn't be sure if I could trust my memory, so father began to make an investigation. It has taken years, but only months ago, when we followed his interest in Anna and then in you, Karl, did we begin to think the time was coming for a confrontation.

"Father went to the FBI and gave them all the information we had collected, not just about the orphanage but many other incidents. As a result, Mr. McDaniels was assigned to us as a kind of special agent. I must confess that for weeks there have been people assigned to follow the two of you, and they came to this conclusion: you were safe when you were apart but in danger when you were together. At first, the thing that prevented Schmidt from attacking you was his absence on weekends, when you were most likely to be together. There was one exception to that schedule. Remember our visit to the Viewpoint Tower, Karl?"

He nodded his head, and an embarrassed grin tugged at the corners of his mouth as he began to understand.

Lisal continued, "That time I was determined to keep you and Anna separated. I was so desperate I deliberately fell down the stairs. I got a little more pain than I anticipated, but as you recall, my fall kept you from being with Anna when the two of you were to have dinner with Schmidt. I am sorry I gave you reason to be irritated with me that night, but I was quite sure Anna was safe as long as you were with me!"

Mr. Schiller broke in. "The night of graduation we were nearly fatally careless. We, McDaniels and I, had become accustomed to Schmidt's leaving on Wednesday nights, and it was only after we'd gotten the report from one of our men that we found he hadn't left town. By then, of course, you were safely back in the city. We picked up his trail the next morning when he was parked down the street from Robert's showroom."

"What?" Anna asked in surprise.

"We began to realize that he knew where you two were as much as we did." He explained, "So from that evening on, you two and alias Smith were never out of our sight.

"We wondered what you were up to when you bought the airline tickets, but we knew you were coming back, because," he paused and grinned, "you and I, Karl, have a dinner date next Thursday. Today, when our men followed you to this unlikely spot, and McDaniels knew Smith was on your trail, we were prepared for a confrontation, a showdown!"

"And I wanted to face him one more time," Lisal added, continuing, "You and Anna were so engrossed in your planning you were unaware I was sitting on the bench that backed up to the one you were on. The high back hid me, and I knew Father and Mr. McDaniels were somewhere in the trees, ready to do whatever might be necessary to protect the three of us. You know the story from there."

Anna said, "I don't know how to say thank you. These past months have been a nightmare and would have been worse if we'd known all this was going on around us. Karl and I couldn't ask anyone for help. We were sure the police wouldn't believe our story, and we didn't want to involve friends because of the danger, so we'd decided to run away for a few days. We were so careful not to let anyone know of the plans. We were hoping Smith would think we'd truly fled. It probably wasn't a wise idea, but it seemed the right thing to do, and we were quite desperate.

The noises from outside the car were the only sounds. A tear ran down Anna's cheek. Karl knew it was not sadness but the beginning of release after months of frustration and years of fear. His own mind was a jungle of questions, and oddly, the question of Mr. Schiller's occupation was uppermost. He had to know what it was that made his work take him away from the city as Schmidt's had done. Karl felt a secret embarrassment that he had suspected him of being one and the same with John Smith. Prompted by these thoughts, he began. "Lisal tells me you are going back to Germany the end of next week. You are finished with your selling trip, then?"

"Yes, my business here is finished for now, but this time we are not going to stay in Germany. We will return to our home on the West Coast."

To cover his confusion, Karl was silent. What did he mean, his business was finished? Did he mean the pursuit of Herr Schmidt? And home to the coast—wasn't their home in Germany?

Lisal had been watching Karl and, laughing, she said, "Father, we owe these two an explanation of your work and our homes. We do have a home on the Rhine River. It is the house that has been in our family for generations, but the only time Father and I return is when we take a holiday. We live south of Los Angeles. Father, would you explain your work?"

They pulled up in front of the hotel. Mr. Schiller took the keys from the ignition and said with a smile, "Inside." They entered the door and turned to go into the dining room. The coolness of the shaded room welcomed the little group. They ordered lunch, and then it was time. Karl leaned back in the chair, looked at Mr. Schiller, and Schiller confessed, "I'm a car salesman."

A look of betrayal and surprise flashed across Karl's face, but Lisal's father chuckled and informed him, "Volkswagens!" How desperately they needed something to laugh about! Schiller explained that he dealt with organizations ordered cars for individuals, and as liaison, he purchased and delivered "bugs."

For a minute the four sat in silence, processing the events in their lives. Lisal broke the reverie. "Father, I think Karl and I need to answer some of your questions." And to Karl she said, "Karl, you've met Father; now would you explain about us." Karl felt everyone's eyes on him while Lisal waited for his declaration. Anna knew it would be a confirmation of what she suspected; she was mercilessly enjoying Karl's discomfort.

Karl jumped at the touch on his shoulder. "Mr. Schiller?" the waiter asked.

From across the table, Mr. Schiller said, "I am Schiller. What is it?"

The waiter said, "There is a call for you, sir."

"I'll be right with you," he responded. And to Karl he said with a twinkle, "This is only a temporary reprieve. I'll be back."

No one spoke while he was gone; each occupied with questions and thoughts touching on the afternoon's events and the present conversations.

When Schiller returned, he informed them, "It was McDaniels, and he'd like all of us to come to his office when we've finished here. Now, Karl, what have you to say?"

This time he was ready. "Mr. Schiller, I love your daughter, and I believe she loves me. We'd like to be married." Lisal put her hand on his, and Anna came around the table and kissed his cheek.

"You have my blessing, Karl. I have no doubt that Lisal loves you, and I believe you return her affection."

Chapter

29

THE THREE CUPS OF COFFEE on Kirstin's kitchen table were cold. The sun had gone down, but Jon wasn't conscious of when he'd reached up and switched on the light.

"Karl, if I hadn't watched you go through this, ignorant as I was, I wouldn't have believed the story," Jon said.

"It's all the truth. That's it," Karl replied, "and you know the rest. The FBI has closed the case on Herr John Schmidt or John Smith. Conrad has given us his blessing for the marriage, and Old Bigelow has given me his blessing for the new job. Anna will be staying on in Denver for a while with Roberts at the car dealership."

"By the way, Karl, what did Anna tell Mr. Roberts about Smith? He must have had questions."

"Funny how that worked out. There was, of course, some question about Mr. Roberts' possible connection to all this secret business, so the FBI came to him. McDaniels told us later it was pretty evident from the first conversation that Roberts was totally in the dark. They told him just enough to help him understand, and it gave him a heart full of sympathy for Anna. He will watch over her like a mother hen. Knowing Anna, this will last about as long as it takes me to tell it. She is an independent young lady, and after all this, she will feel even more qualified to take care of herself. Lisal, her father, and I will leave for the West Coast in the morning, but I want to tell you that it was God's everlasting arms that carried us all these past months. All the things we did not know, all the people who were involved unknown to us, and yet God arranged it all."

"I'll say an amen to that," Jon said.

Finally, Kirstin spoke. "'The Lord is a refuge for the oppressed ... for You, Lord, have never forsaken those who seek You.' That's Psalm 9, an appropriate summary of your life story. I know you are eager to go down the mountain and say your goodbyes to Anna, so we need to let you go, but we will miss you dreadfully."

The three friends walked to the car, and after the goodbyes and godspeeds, Karl backed around, turned the car toward the drive, and switched on the headlights. The beams spread out over the newly graveled lane.

"Take it easy; that much loose rock can be slick as mud," Jon called.

Karl waved his reply as he eased the car down the graveled slope and onto the pavement.

For the first mile he concentrated on the road, but gradually his deep breaths filled the emptiness, and then, out of gratitude, he began to speak.

"Oh, God, how faithful You are. Your eternal promise is that You will never forsake Your own. Oh my faithful God, You have brought me up out of the pit of destruction, out of the miry clay and You, Father, have set my feet upon a rock making my footsteps firm. You have put a new song in my mouth, a song of praise to our God. Many will see and fear, and will trust in the Lord. So be it, my God. Amen."

Epilogue

KARL WAS SURPRISED AT THE small mound of possessions he'd accumulated in the past two years; it barely filled the trunk of his car. He concluded he was leaving much more than he was taking away. From the firm handshake of Bigelow the backslapping at the coffee shop, to the tearful goodbyes at Jon and Kirstin's, and now— how to say goodbye to Anna? In all their growing up and young-adult years, they'd never been more than an hour's distance apart.

As he drove into the car lot, he saw Anna at the window. Instead of hurrying, he slowly turned off the engine, picked up the flowers give her, and forced one foot to follow the other up to the shiny door. Anna hadn't moved. Roberts called out a greeting, and Karl waved a reply.

Wordlessly he handed the bouquet to her. She walked to her desk and laid the flowers on its glassy surface. Turning, Anna said, "Goodbye, Karl." He saw in her eyes and set of her mouth the strength and resolve she'd exhibited even as a child. He watched her for a second and then, stepping forward, put his arms around her. "Dear Anna,"

She hesitated for one breath and then clung to him as she'd often responded in the past. She allowed herself one long sob and then pulled away. "Karl, I'll miss you," she whispered.

He laid his hand on her cheek and said, "Schatz, I'll miss you too."

"Call me when you get to Los Angeles."

"I will," he responded.

"Thank you for the flowers," she said. It seemed a trivial remark, but all the important conversation had taken place the night before, following the trip to the airport with Lisal and her father.

"You're welcome. Are you going to be all right? Are you settled in your apartment?"

"Yes and yes." She smiled as the beginning of a grin touched her mouth. "Karl, I just want to tell you I love you and I'm so happy you found Lisal."

"I love you, Anna. She is pretty special, isn't she?" Karl replied.

For a minute they stood, and then Anna said, "It's time for you to go, Karl."

Instead of another hug, he took her hands, raised each to his lips, and whispered, "Goodbye."

She did not stand at the window as he drove away.

Such a life they'd had. Together they had faced unbelievable danger and misery in the past and recently the threat on their lives. That was over. This was a new chapter.

Karl turned onto Highway 6 and pointed his car west. West—where Lisal was. The word *bittersweet* came to mind. So bitter to leave Anna, his first job, friends, and the mountains, but so sweet to dream of Lisal, a new job, new life and a new city.

Printed in the United States
By Bookmasters